Where on earth was Bob?

"Catherine Seymour and Robert J. Delaney!"

The flat, officious voice of the city hall clerk boomed across the room, startling her. Cathy's pulse pounded. It was time to get married, but where was her groom?

With quivering limbs, she began to stand. A hand clamped down on her arm. "Cathy?"

Startled, she gazed into the deep blue eyes of the hunk sitting next to her. "I'm sorry, Cathy, I can't go through with it," he said in a grave, very audible voice.

A hushed silence fell over the crowded room filled with couples. Holding her arm, the lunatic stood and began to pull her with him. "We need to get you out of here and go somewhere we can talk."

Cathy dug the practical low heels of her pumps into the tile flooring. "I'm not going anywhere with you!" she cried. This strange man was trying to kidnap her! "You're not Bob."

Would she ever be able to convince these people of what was happening? Desperately her eyes darted from face to face and finally settled imploringly on the clerk at the front. "Please," she said. "I've never seen this man before."

The clerk shook his head. "Then all I can say, lady, is if you didn't know the fellow you shouldn't have dragged him down here to marry you."

SUPER ROMANCE

Dear Reader,

Welcome to another wonderful year filled with love and laughter!

First we have a fabulous screwball comedy from the talented Liz Ireland. You may be familiar with her books for Harlequin American Romance and Harlequin Historicals. In *The Hijacked Bride* she's penned a very funny story about a kidnapped bride and her reluctant kidnapper. Hale Delaney certainly never had any idea what he was getting himself into! The dialogue sparkles, the hero is to-die-for and crazy relatives abound. Enjoy!

Then we have new author Barbara Daly debuting with *Home Improvement*. Barbara wowed us with her talent. Her story about the city girl in the wilds of Vermont is a hoot! The characters are charming and warm, the romance is special and the dog, Babe Ruth, is a treasure. I'm not sure how the heroine convinced Babe Ruth to wear all the crazy outfits, but the Babe sure is one well-dressed dog! Discover the fun of home renovations!

Wishing you all the best for a wonderful New Year.

Malle Vallik

Malle Vallik
Associate Senior Editor

THE HIJACKED BRIDE
Liz Ireland

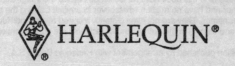

HARLEQUIN®

TORONTO • NEW YORK • LONDON
AMSTERDAM • PARIS • SYDNEY • HAMBURG
STOCKHOLM • ATHENS • TOKYO • MILAN • MADRID
PRAGUE • WARSAW • BUDAPEST • AUCKLAND

ISBN 0-373-44059-6

THE HIJACKED BRIDE

A funny thing happened...

The moment I saw my first Cary Grant movie, I knew what a dream man should be: funny. Naturally, if this funny guy could *look* like Cary Grant, that wouldn't hurt matters, either. But who can resist someone who, when life seems at an absolute nadir, makes you laugh?

Of course, I saw that old black-and-white movie when I was ten. Twenty years later, I would add a few more characteristics to my dream-man list—like an ability to cook, do laundry, wash the dog...and keep me laughing while he does all this!

—Liz Ireland

Books by Liz Ireland

HARLEQUIN AMERICAN ROMANCE
639—HEAVEN-SENT HUSBAND
683—THE GROOM FORGETS

HARLEQUIN HISTORICALS
286—CECILIA AND THE STRANGER
330—MILLIE AND THE FUGITIVE
410—PRIM AND IMPROPER

Don't miss any of our special offers. Write to us at the following address for information on our newest releases.

Harlequin Reader Service
U.S.: 3010 Walden Ave., P.O. Box 1325, Buffalo, NY 14269
Canadian: P.O. Box 609, Fort Erie, Ont. L2A 5X3

For Joe,
who cooks *and* makes me laugh!

1

WHERE ON EARTH WAS BOB?

Cathy Seymour tightly clasped her delicatessen bouquet in sweaty hands. The very appropriate bone-colored suit she had purchased specifically for this occasion felt limp and clammy against her skin; no doubt accordion wrinkles would crease her lap when it came time for her to stand up. Normally Cathy would have rather walked across hot coals than appear untidy, but right now she was so nervous she was beyond caring. She'd been warming up the same city hall bench for the past forty minutes now, and there was still no sign of her fiancé. Her *very reliable* fiancé. Something terrible must have happened to make Bob Delaney forty minutes late for his own wedding!

Bob had told her it was a bad idea to meet downtown, but no, she had insisted. No matter that they were having a prearranged elopement; it was still bad luck for the groom to see the bride before the ceremony. To Cathy, a wedding just wasn't a wedding without some superstition and tradition. She'd never understood couples who could just jet off on a whim to Vegas, to be married in their blue jeans by an Elvis—which, incidentally, was what her parents had done. She wanted something a little more proper, more normal, for herself, even if it was just city hall.

That was a prime reason she was marrying Bob Delaney, who was about as far from the flaky Seymour family as she was likely to get in this lifetime. Bob reeked normality.

Some people might find him a little boring, but Cathy couldn't think of a man she'd rather move to the suburbs with. And that's exactly where they were headed, just as soon as their nest egg was big enough. She could hardly wait. Finally, she would really be living her dream of white picket fences and backyard barbecues. They could join a country club and have a bunch of kids and the greenest lawn in the neighborhood, just like people in the movies and TV commercials... *If* Bob ever showed up.

She felt her mouth go dry as a horrible thought hit her with the force of a two-by-four. Was Bob purposefully not showing up? Could she actually be in the process of being jilted?

Nonsense! Probably something had happened at the bank, Cathy assured herself. If there was one thing on earth that Bob Delaney cherished more than her, it was the FIB— the First International Bank—where they both worked, she as a loan officer and he as one of the vice presidents in charge of international accounts. It was just hard for her to feel too sympathetic for a bank when her future—not to mention nonrefundable honeymoon tickets to the Cayman Islands—were at stake.

A long, sturdy pair of legs appeared before her, pushing the uncertain status of her honeymoon right out of her thoughts. In fact, the startlingly handsome man in front of her managed to exile Bob Delaney himself to a desert island of her consciousness. Slowly, her eyes travelled up the suited body, up slim hips and a broad chest that made the crisp but plain yellow shirt covering it eye-poppingly appealing. The man had a square jaw and a nose that looked as if it had withstood some breakage, giving him a weathered, dangerous look. Finally, she met with the most arresting pair of clear blue eyes she'd ever seen. Her lips parted about the same time her mind made a very interesting observation. This tall, dark-haired stranger was hands down the handsomest man in the room—and he was alone. Not only that, he was looking directly down at her—as if *she* were the one person in the world he was looking for.

Her heart fluttered erratically a few times in response...until she managed to get a grip on herself. *You're about to be married—and so, probably, is he!*

Cathy prided herself on being sensible, so she began to search for some flaw in the man's appearance she might have overlooked, something that would make him seem less desirable—like a budget shopper looking for a flaw in a designer handbag that she couldn't afford anyway. It took some doing, but her eyes zeroed in on that fatal flaw. *His tie!* How had she missed it? It was a ghastly psychedelic striped affair—a fashionable throwback to the 1970s, the decade she'd spent in and out of a commune, and would prefer to forget.

Bad Necktie nodded to the empty space next to her, silently asking if the place was taken. His simple gesture filled Cathy anew with panic. Giving up that empty space—which in a way stood for Bob, after all—would be a little like giving up on her wedding, wouldn't it? Nevertheless, what could she do? Every other seat in the place was filled with happy couples. She scooted over to make room for the handsome stranger. The stranger with the bad necktie, she corrected. At least with another person on the bench with her she would feel less...single.

She surreptitiously glanced at the hunk sitting beside her. Maybe when Bob walked in and saw her waiting in the marriage bureau with another man, it would make him a little nervous.

Then again, maybe not. It wasn't likely Bob would suspect her of eloping with a hunk, not even for a nanosecond.

As he always said, her best quality was her stridently sensible nature.

That, of course, was a matter of perspective. Her sister, Joan, thought practicality was Cathy's worst quality. But then, Joan was almost as nutty as their parents, with the fortunate exception that she managed to hold down a steady job. And like Cathy she lived in New York City, not Guatemala, which was a sensible choice given that she made her living as a therapist.

Cathy was Joan's favorite test case. "Someday," her big sister always warned her, her words inevitably accompanied by some long-nailed finger wagging, "someday that free spirit you've been running from all these years will burst loose, and cause your carefully controlled life to topple like a house of cards."

That thought made Cathy shudder with trepidation. She might have been christened Blossom Drop and raised on a commune, but that was the past. As soon as she was old enough to buy a bus ticket out of Santa Fe, where her parents had been dabbling temporarily in crystal healing, she'd changed her name and transformed herself into the most buttoned-down of the buttoned-down. She'd never strayed.

Well. Except that one little incident with Skippy Dewhurst right after college. Thank heavens Joan didn't know about that! Cathy would never have heard the end of it— when really the whole business was nothing but a slightly humiliating learning experience, one that had steeled her resolve never to make such a dismally fickle life choice ever again. Ever since Skippy, she'd been grabbing for that upper-middle-class brass ring, that suburban nirvana, that dream life with a solid citizen like Bob.

Joan thought her marriage to Bob was an aberration, but Joan was a woman who changed weird boyfriends almost as frequently as she changed her hair color, which was about once a week. Joan, for all her modern ways, truly believed that every woman was a Cinderella, breathlessly awaiting Prince Charming's arrival. And Bob Delaney was definitely not her idea of P.C. According to Joan, by marrying Bob Cathy was kidding herself—"sublimating her romantic nature." But to Cathy, Bob, with his banker's paunch and wire-rimmed glasses and his Connecticut background, *was* Prince Charming, and their castle would be a split-level on Long Island.

Out of the corner of her eye, Cathy looked at her thin gold watch, careful not to alert anyone in the crowded room that she might be an abandoned bride. Bob was now forty-five minutes late. Her face heated with anxiety. Could Bob *really* be jilting her? Steady, reliable Bob?

Never! Bob Delaney didn't know the meaning of the word devious. Oh, maybe he sneaked an extra Snickers bar in the afternoon, or switched to caffeinated coffee in hopes she wouldn't notice, or ducked out to a happy hour with his buddies, when he knew alcohol was bad for him. These were minor infractions, but he certainly wasn't a cad! Nor was he the type to be late.

Cathy bit her lip nervously, feeling a bead of sweat trickle down her spine. She began to fan herself with the wilting daisies and gave her engagement ring a few nervous twists. Could something have happened to him? Should she call the bank?

"Catherine Seymour and Robert J. Delaney!"

The flat, officious voice boomed across the room, startling her. Cathy's pulse pounded. It was time to get married, but where was her groom? Why, oh, why had she given the clerk their names before Bob had arrived? And what should she do now? Should she admit Bob wasn't here, and risk losing their place?

"Catherine Seymour and Robert J. Delaney?" The clerk's face, which had held the same bored, placid expression for forty-eight minutes, now came alive with speculation as he scanned the room. "Are Catherine Seymour and Robert J. Delaney here?"

Couples whispered to each other and looked around in curiosity as Cathy's knees knocked with panic. It would be a long, long lonely walk across that room. But she just couldn't sit here and pretend she didn't hear the man! To do so would make it even more embarrassing when Bob showed up—*which he was bound to do any moment now,* she assured herself.

The clerk's face broke into a smile. "Catherine Seymour and Robert J. Delaney—going once, going twice..."

Cathy attempted to clear her throat, yet the tight marble-sized knot that had lodged there wouldn't allow a sound to come out. With quivering limbs, she began to stand.

A hand clamped down on her arm. "Cathy?"

At the sound of her name, Cathy stopped and a roomful of heads turned in her direction. Startled, she gazed into the deep blue eyes of the hunk sitting next to her—the guy with the bad necktie. In her panic about Bob, she'd almost forgotten he was there. She looked down at the fingers gripped firmly about her arm, then back into the man's blue eyes. Who was he, and how did he know her name? And why was he gazing at her so soulfully?

"I'm sorry, Cathy, I can't go through with it," he said in a grave, very audible voice.

A hushed silence fell over the room. Cathy heard the blood pounding in her ears as she stared into the hunk's earnest face. Was he insane? She tugged on her arm, but he refused to let go.

"P-please," she gasped.

"I was afraid you would beg." He shook his head sadly,

then looked back up at her, his eyes glistening with tears. Tears! "It's not that I don't love you, Cathy."

"You *are* insane!" she cried, finding her voice at last.

The man's eyebrows knit together. "Cathy, please don't make a scene."

It was like *The Twilight Zone.* Or a nightmare. That was it! Maybe she was sleeping, having a bad dream. Bob wasn't late. This wasn't happening. If she just closed her eyes and counted to three...

One, two, three. When she opened her eyes, that blue gaze was still fastened on her, the look of concern deeper than before. "Darling, do you feel faint?" Holding her arm, he stood. "We need to get you out of here...and go somewhere we can talk."

Cathy dug the practical low heels of her bone-colored pumps into the tile flooring. "I'm not going anywhere with you!" she cried. "You're not Bob! Who are you?"

He just shrugged. Unless he really was a madman...and then maybe it wasn't pretend. If that were the case, it was even more crucial not to let him drag her away. Cathy clutched the bench armrest. "I'm not leaving!"

"Darling," the lunatic soothed, "you're making a spectacle of yourself."

It was true. Couples eyeballed the unfolding drama with shock and pity—the would-be bride refusing to leave the scene of the jilt. This *was* a nightmare!

"Someone help me!" she cried, pointing at the stranger frantically with her deli bouquet. "This man isn't my fiancé!"

"Not anymore, apparently," someone quipped.

New Yorkers!

Would she ever be able to convince these people of what was happening? Would anyone care? Desperately her eyes darted from face to face and finally settled imploringly on the clerk at the front. "Please," she said, "I've never seen this man before."

The clerk shook his head. "Then all I can say, lady, is if you didn't know the fellow you shouldn't have dragged him down here to marry you."

"But I didn't!" Cathy practically shrieked. "Will someone please call the police?"

As every single person in the room gaped at her, Cathy felt her body go limp in frustration.

"Honey, honey, honey…" Seeing her weakening, the man dragged her boneless jittery body away from the bench and pulled her close. Cathy pushed against his chest as hard as she could, until she heard him whisper for her ears alone, "I have a gun, lady. Move toward the door, pronto."

Gasping in shock, she stared into his blue eyes as with his right hand he led her corresponding hand down his jacket. A hard lump rested beneath his coat. A hard lump that felt like a gun.

Her hand jerked back reflexively and he smiled. "Ready?"

Oh, Lord… Terror settled into her quivering bones. She could just imagine the headlines. Bloodbath at Marriage Office! Stories of innocent couples on the brink of lifelong bliss gunned down because she was a magnet for weirdos.

Numbly, she nodded. What else was there to do? No one in this building was about to help her. Once out on the street she could make a dash—but for what? Where would she run? And what had happened to Bob? Did some hoodlum have him, too, or was this madman working solo, preying on lone women in marriage offices?

The questions galloped through her mind as she somehow managed to put one foot in front of the other, clutching her flowers and her handbag tightly. As she and the man passed, couples *tsked* at the sight of a wedding-day casualty in retreat.

"You won't get away with this!" she said as they walked through the door into an empty hallway, their footsteps echoing against tile and marble.

"Listen, don't jump to conclusions," he urged.

"What else am I supposed to do—wait patiently to see if I end up at the bottom of the East River?"

He rolled those Paul Newman blues. "I assure you, that's not going to happen."

Right! As they crossed the foyer, approaching the revolving door that led outside, Cathy tried to picture the world outside—a flight of steps, the busy avenue, the graying edifices of surrounding city government buildings, the subway station two blocks away. Where should she flee? The revolving door posed an obvious problem for her captor. She mentally geared up to bolt the minute he let go of her, but he kept a firm grip on her arm and swung her around in front of him. In lockstep, they shuffled into the triangular space, mincing awkwardly until a gust of spring air alerted them to duck out of the door's relentless circular path.

Cathy seized that clumsy split second as the door deposited them outside. Jerking her arm free, she ran hell-for-leather toward the steps, dashing past startled pedestrians with Bad Necktie close on her heels. She could hear his heavier footsteps running behind her, see his shadow cross hers as they raced down the stairs. Next time she got married, it would be in sneakers!

He caught her elbow as they again hit even pavement, and his sudden stop pulled her up short against his chest.

"Let me go!" she cried, whacking his psychedelic tie with her purse.

The man reacted to her blows as if she were a slightly

annoying gnat. "Cool your jets, lady," his gravelly voice said in her ear. He didn't sound the slightest bit out of breath, which angered her even more. "I just need to talk to you."

"Oh, sure! Just want a cappuccino and conversation, I'll bet!" Cathy cast her gaze around anxiously as he tugged her along to the curb. Way over on the other side of the avenue was a policeman. Should she yell, or make another dash for freedom?

They came to a stop in front of the door of a late model sedan. With his free hand her captor opened it and instructed, "Get in. I promise you won't get hurt."

Some promise! And yet, as she looked into the velour interior of the back seat, then again at the policeman across the street, a plan formed in her mind. If she timed it just right...

"All right." She forced her voice to sound pleasant. In response, for the first time she saw her captor's lips twitch into something like a smile. At least, a deep dimple appeared to the right of his lips, making him look as if he were smiling. It also made him heart-stoppingly handsome. Just her luck. The only time she encountered such a gorgeous creature at close range, he *would* have a gun in her side!

Every muscle tensed like a cat preparing to spring, Cathy stepped into the back of the car, noting the driver in front for the first time. She tried to memorize what she could about him for later. Maybe she could recognize his bald spot in a police lineup. As she made contact with the seat, Bad Necktie let go of her arm to get in himself. The moment he did, she vaulted across the seat and launched herself against the opposite passenger door. Ignoring traffic, she jumped out of the car, slamming the heavy door behind her. A cab honked long and hard as it whizzed by her, missing her by inches. She darted out as soon as the cab passed and began sprinting toward the policeman on the other side of the street.

"Help! Officer!" she cried, spurred by the sound of the sedan door slamming shut again behind her. "Officer!"

She ran, heedless of oncoming traffic. Heart pounding, she concentrated only on the blue uniform. As she neared him, the cop's surprised face came into focus.

"Officer!" she cried, panting. "You've got to hel—"

The man's chubby face broke out into a wide, friendly grin. "Hiya, Captain!" the policeman said, tipping his hat genially to someone behind her.

Captain?

Confused, Cathy whirled around. Bad Necktie stood smiling, dimple intact, blue eyes twinkling. "Hello, O'Donnell. Hard day of strolling around, I see."

The cop chuckled. "And I can see now how you spend your days off—chasing pretty women!"

Cathy's jaw dropped in astonishment. *This man—this gun-toting thug—was a policeman?* Her shoulders sagged. This definitely was not her day.

His hand again locked firmly on her arm. "Just a little unofficial business."

O'Donnell, an older man, chortled. "Is that what they're calling it nowadays?"

"No, they're calling it abduction," Cathy said flatly.

Both men laughed as if she'd just made a big joke, and Bad Necktie began tugging her away. "C'mon, Cathy."

O'Donnell winked. "Go easy on him, Miss. He's gentler than he looks." Then he cracked up all over again.

Cathy couldn't keep the scowl off her face. No wonder crime was so high in the city when innocent people could be abducted in broad daylight—in government buildings and right in front of a policeman, *by* a policeman!

Suddenly, a wave of realization nearly knocked her over. *A cop!* Oh, heaven. They'd caught up with her!

She stopped. "Is this about the parking tickets?"

Her captor pivoted, frowning. "Parking tickets?"

She didn't waste any time launching into an explanation. "Because if it is, I'm willing to pay up right now. I would have before, but they really weren't *my* tickets. They were Bob's."

"No, listen, lady—"

"*I'm* a law-abiding, Volvo-owning citizen," she said, knowing she was babbling, but desperate to get herself out of this pickle. "See, we use it on weekends sometimes—"

"Would you be quiet?" he said impatiently as he tugged her across the street. "This isn't a parking problem."

Her brain whirred as it attempted to shift gears. Not a parking problem. What could it be?

"And I have to say, what you did just now was really dumb."

She couldn't believe the nerve of the man. "Well, pardon me!" she snapped back. "My mother always warned me against getting in cars with strange men."

Which was a blatant lie. Her mother, who lived and breathed macramé during Cathy's formative years, had never given her daughters any such practical advice.

Bad Necktie paused as he again opened the car door for her. "Let's get one thing straight, Cathy—"

"How do you know my name?" she interrupted. "Who *are* you?"

To his credit, the man actually seemed to consider answering her question. His strong jaw worked from side to side as he thought. "Never mind. Believe me, you're not going to get hurt—unless you insist on jumping in front of moving vehicles."

"Never mind?" she asked, flabbergasted. "I'm being kidnapped, and you're telling me to *never mind?"*

"Nothing's going to happen to you."

"If you're so harmless, what's with the gun?"

"I'm a cop," he answered.

"Don't try that with me—I watch TV. I've seen enough shows on cops gone bad to know to be scared."

He rolled his eyes. "I was just trying to explain why I have a gun."

"Would you care to explain why you threatened me with it?"

"I needed to get you out of there."

He was a gun-toting goon, was what he was. He—

Just then, a thought occurred to her, and the blood drained out of her face. "You're not...not FBI, are you?"

He tilted his head. "Why?"

Her heartbeat stopped. Of course! "Is this about my parents?" With all the excitement about the wedding, she hadn't been listening to the news much lately. There could have been a coup d'état in Central America that she hadn't heard about, or some disaster that her crazy parents might have become embroiled in. Or worse... Maybe they were back in the U.S...in jail!

"Your parents?"

"Because if it is, I think I can clear up a few details," she said quickly. "They were never really deported, you know. And the only reason they were growing that hemp in the first place was to prove a point about deforestation. Not that *I* agree with their tactics, mind you, but—"

"What?"

"You see, you can make paper from it, and all sorts of useful products—"

"Hemp?" The man looked more confused than ever. "Lady, what the heck are you talking about?"

"My parents," she explained.

"This isn't about your parents, or parking tickets, or hemp, or anything like that," he told her. "It's about your fiancé."

Every muscle in her face went slack and her heart pounded a slow beat of dread. "Bob? What about Bob?"

He nodded to the back seat. "Get in, and we'll discuss it."

"No! I want to see Bob!"

"You will, as soon as you get in the car," he insisted.

Cathy couldn't have said why, but in that instant she detected a note of sympathy in the man's voice, and a little regret. She looked again into his blue, blue eyes and was surprised to see a hint of kindness there. And she was struck anew by this man's appearance. There was something familiar about him...something about the face. Could it be possible that she'd seen him before?

Yeah, right. On a post office wall, maybe!

But maybe Bob was in some kind of trouble—maybe that's why he had been late for their wedding. She had to find out.

"You promise I'll be able to see Bob?" He nodded. "When?"

"Immediately."

Taking a deep breath, she slowly turned and got into the car. He followed, and before they were even fully situated in the back seat, Cathy heard the automatic locks click into place.

"Hey!" she cried, turning on him as though this were a betrayal of their verbal agreement. "Am I a captive?"

Bad Necktie, once again his old unreadable self, ignored her. He faced forward and looked straight into the driver's rearview mirror. "Brooklyn," he instructed.

"Brooklyn!" Cathy protested. "Bob would never go to Brooklyn." Not even at gunpoint.

"You got that right, lady." Bad Necktie turned to her, cynical humor sparking in his eyes. "Bob's not in Brooklyn."

"You lied!"

"No, I didn't."

"Where is he, then?" she asked in growing panic as the car moved forward, then turned onto a side street. "You said I would see him!"

"Look behind you."

For a moment, the car slowed to a stop, allowing Cathy a good look at a black limo at the curb of the avenue they had just pulled off of. There in the back seat, his body turned so that his face was pressed against the back window, was Bob. His wire-rimmed glasses made his blue eyes appear owlishly wide with surprise as he also caught a glimpse of her.

"Bob!" she cried, squashing her face against the glass of the sedan's back window. He was a captive, too! But why? And why in heaven had she ever agreed to get into this car?

Bob's pudgy hands flattened against the glass, and the sight of his cuff links glinting through the limo's lightly tinted window brought tears to Cathy's eyes. He was all gussied up for their wedding! He hadn't been late, after all. Just kidnapped. She called his name again, and, as the limo pulled into traffic, she could have sworn his lips formed hers, too.

"Stop them!" she cried to the man beside her. "They're taking him away!"

"He'll be all right where he's going."

But how could she be sure? She remained plastered against the back window, watching her fiancé recede into the distance until he was no more than a bug-eyed speck. Suddenly, Cathy mourned for the wedding that was supposed to have brought her so much garden-variety happiness. So much normalcy. Perhaps she hadn't looked forward to her marriage enough, at least to the loving and cherishing part. But then, Bob had never seemed quite so dear to her as he was right this moment, being hauled away in an unmarked car.

2

"NAB THE FIANCÉE." Those had been his instructions.

Okay, so maybe he'd screwed up. Hale Delaney wasn't accustomed to kidnapping women from marriage offices, but he hadn't been able to think of any alternative. Now he had to admit his calculations had been all wrong. First, he'd expected his brother's fiancée to be more like Bob. More malleable. More…well, boring. But Cathy Seymour turned out to be feisty and beautiful and a hell of a lot braver than Hale had anticipated.

He felt grim. He was a cop, not a lawbreaker. Not a thug. In fact a part of him—the part that gave safety lectures at public schools and had dedicated a decade of his life to trying to make the streets of New York even a little safer—wanted to lecture her for getting into a car with a stranger. Any stranger, even himself. He let out a breath of frustration. Cathy looked over at him, her dark eyes flashing. He knew he shouldn't say anything to her, but he couldn't help himself. "Do you have any idea what can happen to a single woman all alone in the big city?"

She sent him an exasperated glare that let him know she would have gladly taken his tie and strangled him with it. "Thanks to you, I might just become an expert on the perils of being *single!*"

"I only meant that you need to be careful," he said evenly, trying to do damage control. "You can't trust everybody in New York."

She sputtered. "I'll say! I trusted you for half a second and now look at me—my little Ozzie and Harriet dream-world has been snatched from my grasp."

Hale noted the way she was squeezing the life out of that bouquet of hers. He didn't blame her for being hostile. If she was harboring little white picket fence dreams, this day, courtesy of yours truly, might have put the kibosh on them for good. Nor could he blame her for panicking. He just hoped she wasn't hatching another escape attempt. Her cross-avenue dash earlier had nearly given him a heart attack! Didn't she realize people drove like lunatics in New York City? "You shouldn't run out into the street, either," he couldn't help adding.

"Thanks." The glare intensified. "Next time I'm kidnapped, I'll remember that." She turned her gaze out the window, once again giving him the silent treatment.

This whole situation made Hale feel like a cop on the verge of a nervous breakdown, and he was normally a very easygoing guy. Too easygoing, as his dear old dad might say. Kevin Delaney, an Irish immigrant, expected his sons to live the bustling American dream life he'd struggled to achieve for himself—a career in business, a big house in the burbs, kids. And both his sons, in varying degrees, had disappointed him. Hale couldn't speak for Bob, but his own departure from Dad's philosophy stemmed from the moment he realized that the house and the job and the kids hadn't brought Kevin happiness. Only his marriage had—but Hale had also seen how his mother's early death had torn Kevin apart, and away from his children. Ever since then, the fifties' TV ideal had made Hale queasy—that Ozzie and Harriet business that Cathy had spoken of definitely wasn't in his cards. He tried not to get caught up in any family entanglements.

But here he was, enmeshed in this mess. And why?

Maybe it was just pity. After ten years of rarely talking to him, his father had come to him, begging for help. All Hale had noticed was how old his father looked, and how much it must have cost him to ask his son for aid. Hale had a weak spot for people in need…which, as a cop, was something of a professional liability. He was forever handing out clean hankies and hot coffee to folks with hard luck stories. So no matter that he thought his dad's scheme harebrained; no matter that he had no beef against Bob; no matter that he believed there were more direct ways to go about finding out if Bob was up to something criminal—at Kevin Delaney's request, he'd foolishly agreed to look after Bob's fiancée. Mistake number one.

He glanced over at said fiancée. She was beautiful—his mind returned again to that fact. It stunned him. How had Bob, who'd been considered a nerd even among the protractor set in high school, lucked out? Maybe it was just as the old man had always warned: money was the ticket to the good things in life. Bob's job at the bank meant lots of green stuff—if their father's hunch was correct, maybe even a lot more than Bob was entitled to. And Cathy, with her chestnut hair, slim figure, and brown eyes that a man could dream about, could definitely be categorized as a *good thing*.

Hale shook his head. Never in his life would he have predicted that he'd be jealous of his brother! And he *wasn't* jealous. He wasn't. Not really. Then again, he couldn't keep his eyes off Cathy. And as he looked at her he felt guilty.

Which was ridiculous. As ridiculous as the thoughts that had been going through his head in that marriage office had been. For a few moments, he'd actually allowed himself to wonder what it would be like to have found a woman to share his life with—who would always be there on cold winter nights after he'd worked a late shift. Before, he'd always considered the two most brutal words in the English language to be *permanent relationship*. That was just the initial trap in that humdrum life he'd been avoiding all these years. But taking a sidelong glance at Cathy, he could almost see where all those one-woman guys were coming from.

Of course, it was just his luck the woman sparking this revelation *would* have to be his brother's fiancée. This was not your typical day in the life of Hale Delaney. Already he'd threatened a woman with bodily harm, kidnapped her, lied to a fellow police officer—and now here he was coveting his brother's almost-wife. And it wasn't even suppertime yet!

Out of the blue, Cathy laughed. Hale jumped, surprised by the sharp cackle. Just a moment ago she'd been giving him the evil eye. When he glanced over at her, his gaze quizzical, she was smiling broadly.

"Okay, I get it," she said, clapping her hands together. "This is a big gag, right? Did Bernie Morton send you guys to kidnap Bob and me?"

The detective in Hale, ever alert for clues, latched on to the name. "Who's Bernie Morton?"

She continued smiling, and waved off his innocent question. "That Bernie!"

"Who's Bernie?" Hale repeated.

"C'mon—you don't have to bluff anymore." She laughed again, still shaking her head. "You guys really had me scared!"

"Does he work at the bank?"

She ignored the question. "Where are we going?" She leaned toward him confidentially. "You can tell me. Tavern on the Green? The bridal suite at the Plaza?"

Whoa. If she was expecting any of those swank places, she was going to be sorely disappointed by his apartment.

"Lady," he said stiffly, "I don't want to burst your bubble, but your destination is Court Street, Brooklyn, New York."

As she stared into his eyes, catching his dead-serious expression, the animation drained from her face. "You mean…?"

He shook his head. "It ain't Tavern on the Green," he said, hating but not able to help letting her down again. "Now who's Bernie Morton?"

The disappointment in her eyes hardened to downright belligerence. "As if I'd tell you anything, you…you… bride abductor! What do you have against weddings, anyway?"

Hale was taken aback by the question. "Hey, this has nothing to do with my feelings about marriage."

"You can't care very much for it," she argued, "if you're willing to separate two people just on the verge…of a lifetime…"

In a flash, the steely look in her eye gave way to misery. Her lip quivered, causing a sinking feeling in Hale's chest. *No,* he silently prayed, *please don't…*

Her breathing came in ragged gasps. "…of happiness!" She let out a long, loud wail and began to cry.

Oh God, not this. He couldn't stand to see women cry. He couldn't stand to see anyone cry, especially when he was one hundred percent responsible for their unhappiness. As a cop, he was forever stepping into situations where people were in crisis…and it never failed to tear him apart. Reflexively, he reached into his pocket, dragged out a white handkerchief, and handed it to Cathy.

She shook her head. Her refusal only made him feel worse. He squirmed uncomfortably. Maybe she was right, he thought guiltily. Had his reticent feelings about marriage and fake family happiness made him more likely to jump on board his father's crazy plan for wedding day sabotage?

"All right," he admitted, capturing her attention immediately. She looked up at him with red-rimmed eyes. A little streak of mascara stained one cheek. "Maybe I'm not marriage's biggest fan. All the hoopla about settling down for life with one person, it doesn't seem practical. In my job, I see domestic trouble all the time."

Her lips turned down in a pout and she said hotly, "Bob and I never fight! Never! We both have very even tempers!"

"That's great," Hale said, trying to calm her. "Truly, I hope everything works out for you. Now, please, blow your nose."

He expected more tears. Or for her to turn and look out the window again. He wouldn't even have been surprised if she'd told him to take a flying leap. But what he absolutely wasn't prepared for was the fist that came out of nowhere and slammed against his nose with a resounding *thwack!* Stunned, Hale fell back against the seat.

Cathy's lip curled, and she narrowed her eyes on him. "Take care of your own nose," she said. "It's bleeding."

He looked at his handkerchief, which he'd instinctively dabbed against his face. Damn! She was right—he was bleeding. Probably scratched by that diamond ring on her hand...which was an important fact to commit to memory. Cathy was a lefty.

"That's some even temper you have," he remarked, cocking an assessing glance at her. She looked pleased with herself, as if she'd just put George Foreman to shame. "What do you call that punch—your Harriet Nelson?"

Cathy smirked. "You deserved it, buster."

That was the trouble. He probably did.

He needed to get on the horn to his father. Fast. He didn't want this woman staying at his place one second longer than necessary—he didn't care what that brother of his had done. When he'd agreed to watch over Bob's fiancée, he'd envisioned Bob's future wife as a biddable, shrinking-violet type—a bland nine-to-fiver. Now he had a beautiful, embittered bride to look after, one whose sharp brown eyes—and sharper left punch—made it perfectly clear that she resented the hell out him.

"HOME AT LAST," Bad Necktie said sarcastically as the car came to a stop on what appeared to be the main commercial artery of an Italian neighborhood. The street next to them was chock a block with pizzerias and gelato stores.

Cathy blanched. Italians! Bob hadn't gotten mixed up with the mob, had he?

"Thanks, Tony. You can take her home now."

Oh, thank heavens! Cathy almost wept with joy. She never thought she'd be so happy at the prospect of seeing her tiny one bedroom apartment again. The automatic doors unlocked and she sagged against the seat in relief. Soon this would all be over!

"Aren't you getting out?"

Uncomprehending, she stared into those blue eyes. He'd gotten out on his side and was nodding toward her door.

"But you just told the driver to take me home," she argued.

His mouth twisted in a wry smile. "Not you, Harriet. I was referring to the car."

Being called Harriet did nothing to soothe her bitter disappointment. "Well, you should have made yourself clearer!" she said, facing forward, not moving a muscle. Maybe he'd just let her go if she refused to get out.

He slammed his door and came around to her side. "C'mon, we haven't got all day." When she still didn't respond, he leaned in, grabbed her under the armpits, and dragged her out bodily.

"Hey!" she cried. Despite the fact that they'd tussled before, this was the clearest demonstration so far of how strong her captor was. *Very.* The man must have done some serious weight lifting...or dragged a whole lot of women out of Fords.

She was glad she'd punched him when she had the chance.

He deposited her on the pavement, shut the car door and waved the driver on. As they stood together on the bustling afternoon sidewalk and watched the sedan pull away, Cathy suddenly felt that her connection to her old life had been severed.

"Let's go," the man said.

"Go where?" Cathy demanded, resisting his insistent tug.

"I live here." He gestured to the building beside them. A green-and-white striped awning covered the sidewalk and inside the first floor store window were displayed cakes, platters of cookies and haphazardly arranged baskets of bread.

"You live in a bakery?" Cathy asked.

"I live *above* a bakery, on the third floor. Carlo, the owner, is my landlord."

Cathy frowned. "If you think I'm going into your apartment, you're nuts! I don't even know your name!"

His blue eyes suddenly sparking with amusement, he gave her a mocking bow. "Hi, Cathy, nice to meet you. My name is Hale."

Hale. *Hale and hearty.* She felt her lips attempt to twitch into a smile, but forced herself to remain unamused. "I'm still not going to your apartment."

He let out a sigh. "Listen, I know this seems odd—"

She let fly an unladylike snort.

"Maybe if I told you who I am, you'd—"

"Forget it," she said, hands firmly on her hips. "If you were Harrison Ford, I still wouldn't go up to your apartment."

He grinned. "Really?"

"Well…" This was not the time to get all balled up in hypotheticals. "I don't care what you say, I'm not budging!" Cathy looked down the street and saw a cross-street light change from green to red. Then she glimpsed a subway entrance a few blocks away. In spite of her words about not budging, she took a deep breath and made a break for it.

Before she'd covered ten feet, however, a hand came down on her shoulder, jolting her to a stop. Hale whipped her around to face him. "I can't believe I have to do this."

"What?" Before Cathy could so much as flinch, he hoisted her in the air. She landed over his shoulder. "Hey!" she cried, twisting. He held firmly to the backs of her knees, and was shaking his head, as if she'd forced him to do this. As if this were all *her* fault! Cathy realized that she was still clutching her pocketbook and wilted daisies, which she used now to whack the sturdy arm that had her lower body pinned against his torso.

Hale laughed. "Do you know you have a problem with aggression?"

She rolled her eyes. "Being kidnapped brings it out in me!"

Hale stopped in front of a door and while easily managing his caveman carry fished through his pocket for his keys. They passed through two doors and began to trudge up a flight of stairs.

"You can put me down now."

"It's no trouble," Hale said, continuing on as if she were nothing more consequential than a rolled-up carpet. "You're a guest, after all."

"Guest!" She spat the word. "I'd love to know what other kinds of guests you've had in your cesspool apartment. No telling who might turn up. Maybe even Jimmy Hoffa!"

At his apartment door, Hale put her back on her feet. "Look," he said, jamming his key into the dead bolt keyhole. "Can we cut the melodramatics? I know you don't believe me, but I'm not going to hurt you."

"You're right I don't believe you! What kind of fool do you take me for? If you think I'm taking one step inside your, your...lair, you're nuts!"

He cocked his head as if considering her words. "Not much to do out here in the hallway."

She squinted in irritation at his glibness. Especially since his wry expression caused that tantalizing dimple of his to make another appearance. How could she be even slightly attracted to someone causing her so much grief? "I'm not interested in doing anything except finding out about Bob. Where are you people keeping him? And why?"

"I'm not going to discuss this with you out here, Cathy. Come inside and I'll fill you in on the details."

She crossed her arms. "Absolutely not."

"You won't do Bob much good out in the hallway."

Cathy bit her lip. "Who are you? Do you know my fiancé?"

He hesitated. "You could say I've known him forever."

"Friend or foe?" she insisted.

"I'm just the intermediary," he said, shrugging.

Cathy let out a huff of frustration at his evasiveness. But what choice did she have? Squaring her shoulders, she took a tremulous step inside her captor's dwelling. Hale stepped inside after her, then once again turned the key in the dead bolt. To Cathy's ears, its firm click as the tumblers locked into place sounded like the slamming of jail cell bars.

But as she looked through a short hallway into the living room of Hale's apartment, she suddenly felt more clammy and claustrophobic than if she'd been locked into a dank bare cement cell. Hale drew her forward, into the main room. With each step, Cathy's legs felt more rubbery beneath her. Breathing grew more difficult. It couldn't be…and yet it was true.

In 1988 she had run away from "home," which at times seemed more like a halfway house for Sixties throwbacks, and set out to create a normal life for herself. She'd changed her name and worked her way through college and up the corporate ladder, and most important, she'd found a man whose character she could mold and shape to suit her, and whose dreams of privacy, prosperity, and the good life matched hers. She'd even convinced him to get married. And just when she was teetering on the verge of domestic nirvana, what had happened?

She'd been kidnapped. And worse. Her kidnapper lived in hippie heaven! It was all too much for her.

"I can't stay here!" she cried, panicking. She turned and slammed into Hale's chest, which she beat against as if it were a bolted door. "Let me out!"

He drew back, surprised, but not before she'd landed a few good wallops against his funkadelic tie. "What's the matter?"

She turned, taking in the futon—oh, how she hated those things!—which had a discarded jacket strewn across it. And not only that, it also had pillows strewn all over it. Old pillows with *fringe*. Cathy shuddered, and forced herself to look away. But then her glance fell upon a dirty pair of sneakers that lay on the floor, and trailing up to them, three tube socks. *Three*, which didn't even make sense! There was no table in the room, just an old wooden ironing board doubling as a coffee table. Even so, an old chair that looked as if it had been salvaged from the street appeared to be the receptacle of newspapers and magazines and half-empty coffee cups. Nothing matched. Everything was a jumble.

And then, as if she already weren't under enough strain, what she saw in the doorway leading to the kitchenette nearly caused her heart to stop.

"Beads!" she cried. Very Seventies—just like the main character had on *Rhoda*.

Hale swiveled his head, following her gaze. "What about them?"

"You've got Rhoda beads hanging in your apartment!" she cried, turning on him and shooting him a withering glare deserving of the criminal degenerate he obviously was. "What kind of sicko are you?"

HALE WAS STUNNED. And a little offended. Okay, so maybe he didn't live in *House Beautiful*...and maybe he could have picked the place up a little...but *sicko?* The woman was definitely overreacting.

"Why don't you sit down," he suggested, leading her over to the futon. "You look like you're about to have a stroke."

She flapped her arms away from him. "I *am* about to have a stroke!" she cried, hopping a safe distance away from the futon. She nearly stumbled into a mask that he'd picked up in Mexico hanging on the wall, and jumped away from it, too. For a moment, she seemed to ricochet around the room, nearly knocking over his candle collection, stumbling over his socks, horrified by everything, until she stopped, covering her eyes.

Hale had never met anyone who reacted so violently to interior decor. Her chest heaved with the effort of breathing, like a wild animal caught in a trap. He almost felt sorry for her—except the last time he'd shown any pity she'd punched his lights out. "Look, you seem upset—"

"Upset?" She finally snapped. Her hands came down to her sides and balled into fists, and her pale skin turned a shocking shade of red. "Excuse me? This was supposed to be my wedding day, the happiest day of my life! Right now I should be on a plane to the Cayman Islands for my honeymoon. *My honeymoon!* But no, where am I? In Brooklyn, in your hippie heaven apartment."

Hippie heaven? Hale glanced around his apartment self-consciously. "Hey, maybe the place isn't what you're used to—"

"You have no idea what I'm used to," she said, stopping him.

No, he didn't. But what could he do? A beautiful woman was standing in the middle of his living room, having a full-fledged hissy fit. He felt torn. "Listen, why don't I get you something to eat?"

She took a deep breath and stared at him directly, as though she were wearing blinders that could block out their surroundings. "I'm not interested in food. I'm only interested in Bob. If you're not going to tell me about Bob, and why I'm being held, I demand to know when I can leave."

Hale empathized with her, he really did. He needed to call his father, he thought again. He needed to get this woman out of his hair. "I don't know," he confessed.

Cathy looked at him, dumbfounded. "You *don't know?*" she asked in amazement. "Whoever is in charge of this scheme seems not to have got the organizational knack down yet!"

Hale grimaced. "It all depends."

"On what?"

"On you…and Bob," he said. "And how much you're willing to cooperate."

"Cooperate!" she yelled. "Why should I cooperate with you…you hippie hoodlum!"

He felt his face begin to heat with anger. She had every right to be angry, but for some fool reason, he hadn't expected so much abuse. "Would you please stop calling me that?"

"Which? Hippie, or hoodlum?"

"Both!"

Her brown eyes flashed at him. "You kidnapped me at gunpoint. Your apartment is festooned with beads and fringe and candles. If you can't take the truth, you should stop abducting people and get yourself an interior decorator."

He rolled his eyes, praying for patience. *No doubt Bob's apartment was pristine—like a Pottery Barn ad,* he thought with sudden unexplainable bitterness. He couldn't help it. Something about having his brother's uppity and wildly attractive bride critiquing his haphazard apartment rubbed his fur the wrong way. What had Bob ever done to deserve to have such a pretty, feisty woman in a snit about him?

"Listen, lady," he said in his best tough cop voice, "I'm sorry you've been inconvenienced, and had your tasteful sensibilities offended, but it just so happens that this button-down fiancé of yours could be involved in serious criminal activity."

Her stare changed from exasperated to stunned. "But that can't be!" she protested, sounding genuinely outraged. "The words Bob and criminal don't even belong in the same sentence!"

Yeah, that's what he had thought. At first. Hale's mouth remained a taut line. "There's a pretty good chance that your pillar of virtue is an embezzler."

"That's absurd!" Cathy said. "You can't have any proof—Bob would never do such a thing."

"What about this trip to the Cayman Islands you two were going to take?"

Cathy didn't catch his drift. "Our honeymoon?"

"The Cayman Islands is an international banking center known to be a site for funneling illegal funds."

"It's also a tourist trap," Cathy shot back. "Does wanting to spend a week on the beach make us criminals?"

"No one's said a word against you," Hale told her.

"I'm so relieved to hear it," Cathy said sarcastically, pushing her hair back from her brow. "But you can't have any evidence against Bob, either. I know you can't."

Her brown eyes stared up at him with such blind, trusting sincerity that he couldn't help but crack a smile. "You don't think Bob was going to take you there for *romance*, do you?"

"That's usually what honeymoons are all about," she said, then did a double take, stiffening. "Why, do I strike you as so undesirable that a man wouldn't want to romance me?"

He looked her up and down and nearly groaned at her misunderstanding. Besides having a pretty face, he had a hunch that beneath that unflattering beige thing she wore lay an incredible body. She certainly had great legs. He wondered why, as the possessor of a body most women dreamed of having, she would take pains to hide it from the world.

"Not at all," he answered, letting her know by his head-to-toe once-over that he meant the words. "But c'mon, we're talking Bob here."

She colored at his characterization of her fiancé. "How do you know Bob?"

Hale wasn't sure he was supposed to tell her that information. He had been about to blurt it out before, back there on the street, but Cathy had interrupted him. She'd said he didn't care who he was. Also, he was certain his father wanted to keep this hush-hush as long as possible—inasmuch as the matter involved Delaney *vs.* Delaney.

"You make it sound as if Bob were planning to skip the country," Cathy continued, not waiting for his answer. "But if that's so, why would he go to the trouble of marrying me? Why wouldn't he just go?"

"Maybe he wanted company." He glanced at her appreciatively. "Maybe he realized what a good thing he had and wanted to make his paradise that much more complete."

His words silenced her. Cathy blushed again from the tips of her toes to the top of her head. *So,* Hale thought, *she's not used to receiving compliments.* Old Bob wasn't doing his job right, apparently. Either that or he didn't know what a lucky so-and-so he was.

A smile touched his lips. "It seems to me you don't have much to say in your betrothed's defense."

"Th-there's nothing to defend. Bob is so...so boring!" Cathy's hand flew to her mouth.

"Nice way to talk about your boyfriend," Hale said, unable to conceal a wry grin.

"You made me say it!"

"Me?" He lifted his shoulders innocently. "What did I do?"

"You know very well! None of this makes sense to me—I'm so confused I'm liable to say anything. I don't know what I'm doing here anyway. Am I under arrest?"

"No," Hale said.

"Is Bob?"

He shook his head. "Not as far as I know."

"Then I insist upon seeing him." She lifted her head imperiously and sniffed before adding, "At once."

"You can't."

"I want to talk to him."

"That's not possible right now, either."

Cathy tossed up her hands in the air in frustration. "Then what on earth am I supposed to do?"

A hint of a grin tugged at Hale's lips. "Relax?"

She glared indignantly. "I *never* relax!"

Hale laughed, but he feared she wasn't kidding. "Please, why don't you sit down?"

She didn't look at him. "No thank you," she said in a clipped voice.

Beautiful, but stubborn. Maybe Bob wasn't so lucky after all. "We can't just stand here all day."

"I can."

"Okay, maybe you can," Hale conceded. "But you must want something. I have beer, wine, sodas…"

She crossed her arms over her chest. "I'd like a large garbage bag and a vacuum cleaner."

Hale gritted his teeth. "Listen, why don't you find some music…" He held her shoulders and pointed her toward his stereo. Maybe some tunes would calm her down. "I've got lots of CDs there."

Listlessly, she picked her way across the room and stared at his CDs. Then, after a moment, Hale saw her pale. She stepped back, shaking her head.

"What's the matter?" he asked, wondering what the hell she could have seen in the milk crate holding his CD collection that would make her look as if an Uzi were being pointed in her face.

"Dylan?"

Hale shrugged. "So?"

"I don't care what my fiancé has done," she said defiantly. "I don't care if he's embezzled from the Treasury Department. I will *not* listen to 'Blowin' in the Wind.' You can't make me!"

"Okay, okay," Hale said, "just calm down."

Cathy dropped to her knees and fiddled with the radio knob. She moved it frantically across the FM dial until she reached the classical station. Handel blared out of the speakers. Despite her protests, she *did* seem to relax perceptibly.

Hale nodded. "I like the *Water Music*." When she looked at him skeptically, he protested, "I'm not a hippie. For your information, a girlfriend gave me the fringy pillows."

"Really?" she asked, not believing him. "What was her name?"

He paused at the odd question. What difference did it make? "Her name? I think it was Susan..."

"You *think?*" She looked appalled. "You don't even know for certain?"

"It was three years ago."

"I can remember the name of the man I was going out with three years ago," she replied.

Hale smiled. "Let me guess...Bob?"

She bridled. "I don't see any reason for you to be snide. Just because you live like a sheik..."

Hale let out a sharp laugh. "Listen, I might not be a cheerleader for hearth and home, but that doesn't mean I have a harem at my beck and call. And as for the beads, those are just there because the door is irregularly sized and I'm too lazy to cut a door down to fit."

"Uh-huh."

"You seem awfully young to be a reactionary," Hale said. "I thought most people your age ran around getting their noses pierced."

Cathy wrinkled her nose in distaste. "I'm twenty-eight," she answered brusquely. "And my life experience has been such that I've learned to honor traditional values."

He let out a bark of a laugh. "That was some tradition-bound wedding you and Bob were going to have."

She bit her lip. "My relationship with my family isn't the closest."

"Oh, right," Hale said, remembering. "The ones hiding from the FBI in Bolivia."

"Guatemala." She glared at him. "Anyway, I was raised in a rather unorthodox manner..."

He clucked his tongue. "Ah, I guess that explains your wanting so desperately to become Mrs. Bob."

"Well of course I do! Today is my wedding day!"

"No last-minute doubts?"

"Certainly not!"

For some reason, her answer disappointed him. And intrigued him. She sounded so adamant. Nobody could be *that* sure of herself—except maybe someone who wanted to pattern her life after Eisenhower era television ladies.

Of course, he reminded himself, his brother's fiancée was none of his business. Maybe now was the time to call home. He couldn't imagine what he was going to do with Cathy for the rest of the day. If he called his father and learned that the ordeal was almost over, he could put Cathy in a cab and send her on her merry way.

But when he retreated to the kitchen with his portable phone and dialed Connecticut, the voice that answered the phone wasn't his father's, but that of Swithin, the British butler his father had employed since Hale and Bob were kids. Swithin was more than just a servant—Kevin Delaney relied on his opinion a great deal. For instance, it was Swithin who had gone to the trouble to look into where in the bank the theft was coming from, and had reported his suspicions about Bob. It was also his big idea to have Bob kidnapped in hopes that he would confess. After all these years in their employ, Swithin was just as anxious as anyone to keep the Delaney name out of the papers.

"Ah, Mr. Hale." Swithin's clipped English accent greeted him without any discernable emotion. "Your father is unavailable at the moment, as he's busy interrogating your brother."

Hale laughed. He could only imagine what his brother was going through. His father wasn't exactly renowned for kindness and understanding. "Has the old man tried straight pins under the toenails yet?"

Swithin was not amused. "I don't think matters have reached so desperate a point yet, sir."

But Hale knew that an hour's "conversation" with dear old Dad could make a little Khmer Rouge-type torture seem like a cakewalk. "Well, tell him that if he needs any help getting information out of Bob, I know a guy who retired from the KGB because he thought they'd gone soft. Now he's NYPD."

"I'll keep him advised, Master Hale."

Hale's mouth pulled into a grin. Swithin was as unflappable as his father was excitable. "And you might tell him to call me, immediately."

"Yes, sir."

Hale hung up the phone and walked out into the living room, where Cathy fixed him with a horrified stare. Her face was as white as a sheet. "KGB?" she squeaked, taking a step backward. "*Straight pins* under his *toenails?*"

3

"LET ME PUT IT TO YOU this way. Have you ever heard of a mad terrorist feeding his captive Chinese delivery?"

Cathy focussed on Hale's innocent expression as she finished chewing a steamed dumpling. True, he didn't *look* like an insane torturer—not while he was presiding over an ironing board overflowing with white cardboard containers. But he hadn't *looked* like a kidnapper, either.

"More moo shoo?" he asked, tilting a container in her direction.

She shook her head. She was stuffed. She didn't usually overindulge this way, but food was the only thing Hale had been able to offer her to calm her down. Against her wishes, he'd even lit a few candles, which even she, much as she hated candles, had to admit lent the place an appealing, soothing quality. She'd needed a little calming after she'd overheard the snatch of conversation about the KGB and the toenails, which, if it was a joke, as Hale insisted, she didn't find very amusing.

Poor Bob. Was *he* being fed Chinese food? The salt content was terrible for him, but he would enjoy it. Was he being fed bread and water even? Food meant a lot more to him than it did to her. Too much, she sometimes thought. He was forever wanting to duck into bakeries, or gourmet groceries for a quick bite, or delicatessens to stare at cheeses. On television, his idols were Martin Yan and Julia

Child. He tended to get a little hysterical without three squares a day, plus snacks.

Cathy swore then and there that if she saw Bob again, she would never nag him about food. He could eat blinis all day if he wanted to. She wouldn't say a word.

Hale was watching her, and Cathy realized that was because, unthinkingly, she had been staring at him. Of course, it was hard *not* to stare at a person stretched out on the floor in front of you like a statue of a Greek god reclining. The flickering candles only added to the effect, the shadows accentuating his strong jaw and the planes of his face. Cathy insisted on sitting on the chair while eating, but Hale had opted for a more casual approach. In fact, while waiting for dinner, he had changed out of his suit and psychedelic tie and put on a pair of old striped shorts and a faded purple T-shirt, which had green letters proclaiming across his chest Radnisky's Deli—Good Eats!

His wasn't exactly Greek god attire, and such apparent lack of understanding of the concept of neutral colors was the one factor that helped Cathy keep her thoughts in order. For if truth be told, she found Hale's good looks and slightly teasing manner as maddeningly appealing as they were irritating. But she could never be truly attracted to a kidnapper, especially one who didn't match his clothes properly.

He smiled. "Well, then I guess all that's left is the fortune cookies."

"You can have mine."

Hale gaped at her as if she'd just spoken heresy. "You don't want your fortune cookie?"

"Empty calories," she replied.

He'd been on the verge of tearing open one of the cellophane wrapped cookies as she spoke, and now, with a smile aimed straight at her, he ripped the plastic, pulled the cookie out, broke it, and popped one half into his mouth. She'd never known watching someone chewing on a crunchy fortune cookie could be such a sensual experience. The man made empty calories tempting.

Which was a problem. If there's anything Cathy knew, it was that the flaky Seymour blood ran thick in her veins no matter how hard she'd diluted it with common sense. She had to be vigilant in resisting certain temptations—the biggest of which was good-looking charmers like Hale. As her terrible experience with Skippy Dewhurst at the tender age of twenty-two had proven beyond the shadow of a doubt, she was highly susceptible to charm. So much that she could throw good sense, substance and stability out the window. After Skippy, she'd spent six long years searching for the perfect man. And she'd found him. Bob. She needed to keep her mind on Bob. Poor Bob.

"Listen to this," Hale said, reading the fortune, "'Your life will be turned upside down.'"

Cathy buried her head in her hands. "That was meant for me!"

He looked up, concerned. "Is something wrong?"

She almost laughed. "Yes! My life has been turned up-side down!" The world had to be topsy-turvy if she could lust after someone for the way he ate a cookie.

One dark eyebrow shot up on his forehead. "Bob really means that much to you?"

"Of course! I was about to marry him!"

"Yes, but he can't mean *everything* to you—you must have some life apart from Bob. Don't you have a job?"

"I work at the bank where Bob works," she answered stiffly.

"Hmm... What do you do at the bank?"

"I'm a loan officer—which means I know perfectly well when I'm being interrogated!"

He gave her one of those slow, sexy smiles of his. Something about the way the man twinkled at her made her feel as if some exotic, hyperactive butterfly were trapped in her stomach. "You don't like people looking too closely at your life, do you?"

What a silly question! "Would you?"

He gestured to the room around them. "What you see is what I am."

"A cop with haphazard ideas of decorating and apparently no cleaning lady," Cathy guessed. "You already admitted you don't want to get tied down by one woman."

He nodded. "Correct."

More interested than she cared to admit, she looked more carefully around the apartment, discovering a notable lack of pictures. No family photos...and no girlfriends, either. "I assume you have family somewhere, though you can't be too close to them. This is an apartment no mother could love."

His smile faded. "My mother died when I was little."

Cathy paled, and immediately felt remorseful. "I'm so sorry. Of course I didn't know..." She had never embraced her own family—had been running from them all her life. But she had always had the option of their being there, at least at the end of a long-distance phone line.

"It's okay," he said, forcing a smile.

But it wasn't. In that flash of an instant, she'd seen the pain of loss in his face—he'd looked like a forlorn little boy. She wanted to reach over and hug him, and give him some kind of words of comfort. But that was ridiculous...he was her kidnapper, the cause of all her troubles!

"I have other family," he said, obviously trying to reassure her. "We just don't interact much. I try not to get involved...."

His words trailed off and he again went silent, making

her wonder what kind of troubles he'd seen in the domestic sphere. She scooted over, leaned close and assured him, "I'm the same way with my folks, except of course that I have one nosy psychologist sister who wouldn't dream of letting me get away from her. I'm her favorite head case." She frowned thoughtfully. "And even Bob, who's absolutely perfect in every other sense, doesn't seem to get along with his family very well. At least, he doesn't talk about them."

When she looked back at Hale, his eyes were fastened on her with such intensity that she felt startled. He was so near she could smell his male scent—his piney aftershave mingled with the smell of bayberry candles and black bean sauce. She could feel the coiled strength of Hale's muscles. He was so strong and good-looking, and yet so strangely vulnerable at times, she could have sworn that there was almost a magnetic pull between them. If she turned and leaned just a little closer toward him...

She pushed that shocking idea out of her head. Was she really thinking this way about her kidnapper? Surely not! So he was good-looking—so were a million other men. So was Skippy Dewhurst. But even Skippy Dewhurst hadn't made her heart palpitate. And, technically, he hadn't done a horrible thing like kidnap her, either. Maybe that in itself was the problem. Her sister Joan—who, granted, was a flake, but was also a doctor of psychology—had told her once about a phenomenon, Stockholm Syndrome, in which prisoners grew to love their kidnappers. Perhaps she was falling prey to that illness.

"Cathy?"

She felt Hale's hand touch her arm, which sent her shooting to her feet. Good grief! What was the matter with her?

He looked at her quizzically, but spoke in the same soft voice. "I thought we could talk..."

"Talk!" she exclaimed, as if he'd just suggested something outlandish, like an impromptu game of ice hockey. "We've done too much of that already. Right now, I just want to see Bob."

She didn't want Hale to think that he was making her forget her fiancé for one single second, because he wasn't. He absolutely wasn't.

He sat back on his heels. "But you can't."

She folded her arms. "Then I would at least like to know what he's done."

A dark eyebrow raised with interest. "I thought you were positive that he couldn't have done anything."

"What you *think* he's done, then."

He continued to stare at her, his face expressionless. "Have you ever heard of salami slicing?"

"Of course, but what could that possibly—" Cathy stopped, feeling as if someone had just punched her in the gut. *Salami slicing,* when used in the context of banking, referred to an employee skimming money out of clients' accounts in small increments, and depositing it into another account, usually one owned by a fictitious person cooked up by the crooked employee. As opposed to the acts of accountants who suddenly went berserk, cleared out clients' accounts, and ran off to the Bahamas, salami slicing was a calculated, time-consuming way to embezzle funds. It would take a cool head and a soul impervious to guilt.

"Bob would never do that," she said emphatically.

"What if I told you someone has evidence?"

Cathy shook her head adamantly. "Then I would tell you that they're wrong. I don't even want to discuss this."

"*You* were the one who said you wanted to know what Bob had done," Hale said.

She stood up, her limbs shaking. "And now I know—

and it's preposterous. If I'm not going to be allowed to see Bob, or talk to him, I might as well go to bed.''

His eyebrows rose in surprise. "It's not even six-thirty yet.''

"Yes, well…it's been a long day.'' As she spoke, she suddenly realized how bone-weary she actually felt. The strain of normal marriage jitters mixed with abduction terror had taken more than a typical day's toll on her nerves.

To his credit, Hale looked almost sorry for her. "The ringleader of this thing is supposed to call me,'' he said. "It might be any minute now.''

"Yes, but it might not be till tomorrow." Or God forbid, next week. "I'm going to hit the hay." She nodded towards the white cardboard containers. "Can you handle the dishes?''

"Naturally. You *are* a guest, after all.''

And as she was a guest, a toothbrush was provided. Courtesy of whom? Cathy wondered as she loaded the bristles with mint-flavored paste in the bathroom a few minutes later. The fleeting idea that Hale kept extra toothbrushes around for women who just happened to be spending the night made her uncomfortable. But what else would she expect from the man who couldn't remember the name of the woman he'd been going out with three years ago! In that respect, Hale reminded her of her father, who had flitted from "chick'' to "chick'', while her mother had merely meditated until his midlife crisis had passed. Cathy wondered how often Hale's fringe-pillow girl had spent the night.…

Don't be a nitwit! She began to brush her teeth vigorously, reminding herself that she didn't care who Hale whatever-his-name-was had spending the night. Her brush stopped in mid-stroke. What *was* his name? She examined the monogrammed guest towel he had laid out. Obviously, it had been a gift. Hale didn't strike her as the type who would buy satin-edged hand towels in tasteful hunter green. She looked at the thin embroidered letters: *KHDIII.*

Hale the hostage-taker was a third? Her curiosity grew stronger, and she quickly opened and inspected the medicine cabinet, which was surprisingly absent of all the vices of most people; there were no stray cotton swabs or expired prescription drug containers. Just shaving stuff, Band-Aids, aspirin and the like, all lined up neatly along the three shelves. He definitely won her approval in the area of neat medicine cabinet keeping. No more extra toothbrushes, either, she noted with pleasure before remembering she wasn't supposed to care.

She tried to concentrate on poor Bob, in captivity. How could anyone think Bob—earnest, plodding Bob—was involved in anything even remotely shady? It just didn't make sense!

Except for one thing. That trip to the Cayman Islands. Hale was right; Bob *wasn't* the type for romantic beach vacations. In fact, their original plan had been to go to Philadelphia, and maybe out to Amish country, something that seemed a little educational. But at the last minute, Bob had changed their plans, announcing that they were going to the Cayman Islands. Why? And why did anyone suspect him of anything in the first place? What on earth had Bob gotten them into?

She immediately shook the recrimination from her mind. Bob had done nothing. Yet as she stood looking out the tiny opaque glass bathroom window, doubts recurred. Bob always carefully guarded his privacy. He had an unlisted number. He eschewed gossip, especially around the office. In every way, Bob was the model employee, and his unimpeachable behavior had been rewarded with regular promotions, salary increases, and widening of responsibilities—all of which, incidentally, added up to more freedom of access to accounts and computer records.

Stop it! she admonished herself. Bob was a dedicated worker. The FIB meant everything to him. Probably he was the most hardworking man they had. Hadn't she spent many a lonely night feeling as if she had been widowed to that bank? Many was the Saturday, too, that Bob would go to work all day to clear off his desk. Why, he'd even told her that sometimes he was the only person in the whole building....

A cold chill shivered down her spine. *Oh, Bob,* she thought mournfully. Could it be true? *Criminal activity. Salami slicing.* Hale's phrases echoed in her mind. How much money was involved? And did this make her an accomplice? She thought guiltily of the airline tickets in her carry-on bag, which was just inside her apartment door. Had she been on the verge of flying off to become Mrs. Bob Embezzler?

No! she thought emphatically. She hadn't seen one shred of evidence against Bob. A man was innocent until proven guilty. If his own fiancée didn't stand by that principle, who would?

The trouble was Hale. He was confusing her with his blue eyes and Chinese-by-candlelight. Making her suspect Bob. She needed to get out of there. She needed to find Bob.

She was so intent on her thoughts of Bob, she almost missed noticing the window she stood in front of. It was a small rectangular opening with frosted glass, but, checking it very gingerly, she discovered that the bottom pane actually slid up.

Heart beating wildly, Cathy ducked her head out the window. Below her and to the right was a corner of the fire escape—if she was very careful, she could swing over, then simply walk down to freedom. What luck! The window would be just wide enough for her shoulders; probably Hale had considered the opening too small to be a possible exit.

She leaned back in and listened for Hale, who, by the sounds of water running in the kitchen, was still busy cleaning up dinner things. She didn't have much time. Quickly, she poked her head back through the window and began pulling herself out.

Squeezing herself out, was more like it. After shimmying her shoulders through the narrow opening, things went fairly smoothly until her hips got stuck. Jammed! Panic set in. She couldn't even put her rear into reverse—she was lodged in that window so tightly the fire department would have to come tug her out, or cut the window out around her, or something equally mortifying. Now she knew how a cork felt.

She also began to realize that her initial reckoning of the distance to the fire escape had been overly optimistic. It was farther down, and farther to the right, than she had at first estimated. Which meant that, if she ever did wriggle loose, she was going to have to perform at least two Tarzanlike swings to get to the fire escape steps.

Before she could let this new dilemma soak in, however, she heard the sound she'd dreaded. A knock.

"Cathy?" Hale's voice called from the shut door behind her. She could barely hear him. "Are you still alive in there?"

"I'm taking a shower!" she yelled back.

"What?"

She sucked as much breath as she could squeeze into her diaphragm, given her tight circumstances, and hollered again, "A shower! I'm about to take a shower!"

"For God's sake—are you crawling out that tiny window?"

"No!" she screamed, but at that exact moment, Hale began rattling the doorknob, then pounding against the door. She heard a crash—and then a sound that made her freeze. Hale's laughter.

"Where the hell do you think you're going?"

Her face felt hot with embarrassment. No telling what the view of her looked like from his angle! A surge of adrenaline made her push with all her might, but before she could move a millimeter, two strong hands grabbed her ankles.

Damn! Could nothing go right this day?

"I'm pulling you back in," he warned.

"Good luck!" she hollered back.

He gave her a tug. "Are you…?"

"Yes!" she finished for him. "I'm stuck!"

Hale chuckled, but in a show of force that shocked her, he grabbed her by the calves and dragged her backward. Even her hips began sliding back. Cathy tried to resist, gripping the windowsill for dear life, but his pull was so strong she felt as if she might just stretch out of shape like a Gumby toy. Finally, he gave a mighty tug that caused her to fly backward as easily as a dust speck being sucked through a vacuum hose.

Hale caught her up in his arms. She slammed against his hard muscled chest and drew in a breath as she looked into those sexy, mocking eyes of his. She didn't like the intimacy of the position—or the fact that he had thwarted her escape.

"That was the second time today you could have gotten yourself killed!" he scolded.

He had a point, but at the moment, she didn't care. She had been ready to jump out that window to get away from him, and here she was, closer to him than ever. And he was still acting as if *she* were responsible for her predicament.

"And to think—I used to like cops!" She huffed in frustration, trying to make her weight as heavy as possible. Serve him right if he threw his back out! "Why don't you arrest Bob and me if you think we've done something wrong?"

"Because we're not sure," Hale said as he padded down the hall toward the living room.

"Who is *we?*" she cried. "And who are you? If you think I won't press charges once I'm out of here—"

"You won't," he said as he plopped her down onto the futon.

"Don't be so sure," she warned. "I'll sue you for mental anguish or whatever they call it. And there's no telling what this whole experience is doing to poor Bob's ulcer."

"Look, I'm not supposed to do this, but since you're so hell-bent on killing yourself rather than staying put, maybe this will change your mind." With a sigh, he reached inside his jacket pocket, brought out a very official-looking police badge, and flashed it in front of her face. It was his picture, all right. Those blue eyes were devastating even in a crummy pocket photo. But it wasn't his face that captured her attention. It was his name. Captain Hale Delaney.

Her brows knitted in confusion. "That can't be," she said. "You're really Hale *Delaney?*"

He nodded.

"Then…" She took a deep breath. "Are you a cousin, or—?"

His mouth once again became a thin grim line. "Not a cousin, Cathy. I'm Bob's big brother."

4

"BOB'S *BROTHER?*" Cathy stared at him, her mouth agape.

But of course! Now that she thought about it, he even looked a little like Bob...a muscled-up, handsome-as-the-devil version. No wonder she'd found Hale less threatening than she should have. She'd been kidnapped by a future in-law!

A wave of relief washed over her. Hale wasn't a deranged maniac or terrorist. And no wonder she had been staring at him all afternoon, and had even considered him attractive. It wasn't Stockholm Syndrome. Hale had simply reminded her of her fiancé. Her confused feelings had all been about Bob.

At least, it made her feel better to think so...

"It's not surprising that Bob wouldn't have mentioned me," Hale explained. "I'm not my family's most esteemed member."

That little-boy-lost look was back, and there was a trace of regret in his voice that made Cathy want to give him some comfort. She knew that black sheep feeling well. "Bob never told me about *any* of his family. I've never met your father, or visited your house, or even seen pictures."

Hale went into his bedroom and reappeared moments later with a large vinyl photo album. He plopped down next to her on the futon, placing the photo album in her lap.

Out of deference to Bob, she hesitated to open the album.

Bob must have had some reason to conceal his family life from her, just as she didn't dwell on the details from her own strange family. All the while she was growing up, she'd fantasized that there had been some dreadful mistake at the hospital at her birth, and that her real parents—the Rockefellers, perhaps—would someday fly out to Santa Fe and save her. Maybe Bob felt that way, too.

But why? Curiosity got the best of her, and she turned the album to a page in the middle. The first picture she saw made her laugh. It was a picture of Hale and Bob as teenagers. The two of them were in a two-seater sports car parked along a manicured gravel drive in front of a palatial manor house—Hale, the elder, was in the driver's seat, waving at the camera. It seemed especially odd to see Bob, who could only have been fourteen or fifteen, with the same wire-rimmed spectacles, same pudgy cheeks, same sheepish smile. Likewise, Hale was already a hunk.

"Were you on vacation? This looks like England."

"England?" Hale blinked at her in surprise. "No, that's home."

Cathy froze and looked again at the mansion in the background. "You mean, you and Bob grew up in *that* house?"

Hale nodded nonchalantly. "It's actually bigger than it looks."

Cathy had to clear her throat to speak. "Oh?" It already looked like a place Queen Elizabeth would be proud to hang her hat in. "Bob told me your family was in the beverage business." She'd always envisioned a bottling plant....

"Have you ever heard of Delaney Ale?" Hale asked.

Who hadn't? Cathy was stunned. "You and Bob are *those* Delaneys?"

He nodded, then smiled. "Bob's been holding out on you?"

"He never even hinted." Cathy took a deep steadying breath. "Why would Bob keep all this from me? And why is his own family kidnapping him?"

"Someone's been embezzling from the family trust money held at the FIB."

"But not Bob! I don't believe it!"

Hale nodded. "My father couldn't believe it, either. Both Bob and I have had our disagreements with the old man in the past, but he didn't think either of us would be involved in something like this. That's why Dad didn't go directly to the authorities."

"Thank heavens!" Cathy exclaimed, then realized how that must sound to Hale's ears. "Not that Bob would have been found responsible for any of this…" She shook her head. "In fact, doesn't what you just told me indicate Bob is innocent? Why would he steal the fortune he's already heir to?"

"He's not. Neither am I. Both of us had a falling out with Dad when we chose not to go into the ale business." He shrugged. "Actually, we were disinherited."

"How terrible! Doesn't your father believe in free will?"

Hale laughed. "You have to ask this about a man who had you kidnapped?"

"But this is all a mistake," Cathy said. "Surely if your father *did* march into the bank and demand that they look into the matter—"

"That's not Dad's way," he reminded her. "Especially not when family is involved. He doesn't want to involve outsiders if he can help it. I suppose he thinks he's doing Bob a favor by giving him a chance to cough up the money."

"*If* he has it. Which he doesn't." She thought for a moment. "Bob's in Connecticut, then?"

Hale answered her with a nod. The thought of Bob being

dragged off and interrogated brought back her ire. "I hope he says nothing!" she said. "Who do you people think you are, kidnapping your own relative on his wedding day!"

"That was supposed to be to his advantage, so he wouldn't be missed at work."

"And what about me? How did I get mixed up in all this?"

"Dear old Dad thought that since we were going to be interrupting the nuptials, we might as well try to get a little leverage out of it."

"Your father sounds like quite a guy," Cathy said, crossing her arms in disgust. "No wonder Bob never told me about any of you! The Delaneys must be the most dysfunctional family I know outside of..."

Of *mine,* she almost said, but kept her trap shut.

"Yeah, well, we're not the Cleavers," Hale admitted, then smirked. "Or the Nelsons."

She chose to ignore the crack. "So I assume right now Bob is being told that I'm being tortured or something, just so he'll confess to a crime he didn't commit."

Hale's eyes widened in surprise. "You're still defending him? After he lied to you?"

"He didn't lie," she retorted. "He may have omitted some information, but I don't suppose you blurt out your family history and your bank balance to every girl you date, either."

"No, but then again, I've never asked a woman to marry me."

Cathy couldn't say why she was glad to know that tidbit, but she filed it away with no small amount of interest.

Hale watched her for a moment with those disarming eyes of his. "Look, I didn't want to get involved with any of this," he said at last. "I only agreed to keep you out of the way for a day or so, so you wouldn't start filing missing persons charges.''

Relief washed over Cathy. Relief and anger. "A day? Why didn't you just tell me all this right away!"

He arched an eyebrow at her. "You mean I should have told you very politely, 'Excuse me, ma'am, I'm kidnapping you for a limited time only'? I don't think you would have accepted that.''

"I would have preferred it to thinking my life was in danger!''

"You weren't until you ran out into the middle of traffic and started jumping out windows—"

"Because I thought you were going to dump me in the East River!'' she cried. "If you had just told me you were Bob's brother—"

"You didn't even know Bob had a brother," he reminded her.

Cathy harumphed. But she felt a hundred percent more relaxed now that she knew she wasn't going to be stuck in Brooklyn forever. She wasn't nearly as worried about Bob, either—especially after getting a load of the fortress he was being held in. His prison was certainly more posh than hers.

But I bet the view isn't as good, she thought, idly ogling Hale's profile.

Her gaze darted away from Hale as she realized what an abhorrent turn her mind was taking. Was she insane? One day alone with a man—her wedding day, to boot—and she was mooning over him like a teenager with raging hormones!

"Cathy, I'm sorry.''

Hale was studying her intently. She was sorry, too. Sorry she had met Hale under such odd circumstances. Sorry she was engaged to his brother...

The last thought shocked her, and she put it out of her mind as quickly as possible. It was just the stress talking…

"I've never kidnapped anyone in my life," he continued. "If it's any consolation, I'll admit something to you."

The huskiness in his voice made her doubt that she actually wanted to hear this little confession. She swallowed. "What?"

"I always laughed at Bob," he said, scooting closer to her. "Never in my life did I think I would envy him."

For a moment she thought she would drown in those blue, blue eyes. Never had she felt as if every drop of blood moving through her veins were boiling hot…until now. Hale was looking at her in the most bold, startling way— the same way she sometimes wished Bob would stare at her. But she couldn't imagine a glance from Bob creating such a firestorm of confusion inside her. She didn't know what to say, or where to look—not that she had any choice. Her gaze was locked on to Hale's blue eyes as if he were a turbaned snake charmer and she a cobra weaving woozily in front of him.

And then he bent forward. The movement was almost imperceptible, but Cathy felt it—and felt herself moving toward him, too. Her tongue darted out to wet her lips in anticipation. His hot breath whispered against her skin, and his hand reached down to cover hers. The moment his fingers touched hers, she felt the pressure of her engagement ring pushing into her skin.

At that reminder of her absent fiancé, Cathy shot off the futon like the space shuttle on takeoff. She fanned herself nervously with her hand. In another second she might have been kissing her fiancé's brother! Suddenly the dim room, with its smell of scented candles, felt unbearably claustrophobic. She needed air, she needed to get out of this intimate atmosphere…she needed to get away from Hale.

Men like Hale were for people like her sister, who believed a woman could live on looks alone. Joan would say Hale was a real catch, Prince Charming riding in at the last moment to rescue Cathy from making a boring marriage. But that was silly. Hale was a marriage-hating bachelor who sneered at all her carefully laid plans for the future. Hale was tailor-made for a fickle woman who valued qualities such as unpredictability, charisma, mystery and blatant, raw sexiness.

For a moment, as she stared at him, sucking deep, deep breaths of heavy air into her lungs, she tried and failed to call Bob's face to mind. Oh, this was terrible! She needed to get a grip. She needed...Bob.

"This is all wrong!" she told him, backing away from him until she bumped into the ironing board coffee table. Looking at it sent a shiver through her. It didn't go with the futon. Nothing here matched! Not the furniture, or Hale's clothes, or herself and Hale together. Her mind, which was already working on an order deficit today, craved something uniform and solid. *Oh, Bob!* she thought woefully.

"I'm sorry we met this way, Cathy," Hale said. "I wish there was some way I could make it up to you."

She realized things were even worse now that he was trying to be nice to her—just the gentle timbre of his voice made her want to run over and throw her arms around him, which she absolutely couldn't do. If she so much as touched him, she had a feeling they would both end up falling in a heap onto that futon!

"You *can* make it up to me," she said, trying to shake the mental image of them entwined in the candlelight.

"How?"

"Take me to Connecticut."

Clearly, this was not the answer he expected. *"Now?"*

"If I went there and spoke with your father, I know I could make him see that Bob had nothing to do with the missing money."

Hale grunted. "You don't know my dad. He's not that easy to deal with."

She crossed her arms. "So I've gathered. If a man is willing to kidnap two people on evidence some accountant cooked up—"

"The accountant was telling the truth," Hale said.

"How do you know?"

"Because Dad fired him. If Dad had thought the man might be wrong, he wouldn't have fired him."

Cathy's jaw dropped involuntarily. "You mean he *fired* a man just because he'd done his job well and found a discrepancy in the books? That's terrible!"

"That's Dad. He doesn't want to be told something unpleasant—and he doesn't want bad family news going out of the family."

She shook her head. "Well, never mind. I'm sure I can handle him if Bob and I just sit down with the books and try to get to the bottom of the situation."

Hale sighed. "And you're sure you want to go tonight? You can't wait?"

She took a step backward as he stepped forward. "I want to see Bob!" She knew she sounded like a petulant child, but she couldn't help herself. If she had to stare at that broad chest beneath that purple T-shirt for another second, she couldn't vouch for what would happen. That thought alone nearly reduced her to hysterics. "I need Bob!" she bellowed, collapsing onto the ugly chair next to her. She punched a fist into a fringed pillow and felt her shoulders quiver with repressed sobs.

When she finally glanced at him, Hale's strong jaw was working back and forth uncomfortably. He looked as if he were almost in pain. "Okay, okay, calm down," he said, holding in some emotion she couldn't quite discern. Was it anger...disappointment? "I'll take you to Connecticut. I guess you'll just have to find out for yourself."

"THIS HAS TO BE THE MOST uncomfortable thing I've ever ridden in!" Cathy exclaimed, glancing with distaste around the dark interior of Hale's Jeep.

It was true; she looked incredibly uncomfortable, but that was partly because she was hunched against the window, obviously trying to get as far away from him in the small vehicle as she possibly could. That fact in itself rankled Hale. Did she think he was going to attack her?

He was feeling more frustration than he should for a man who had come a hairsbreadth away from kissing his brother's fiancée. He should have been relieved to be taking her to Connecticut, where he could drop her off and tell his father he was disentangling himself from the whole Bob mess. Instead, he was annoyed.

"Why is the passenger seat on the wrong side?" she asked.

"It's an old postal vehicle. You can pick them up for a song at government auctions."

She looked at him as if he were mad. "And this thing will actually get us to Connecticut?"

"I sure hope so..." Hale said, intentionally injecting a doubtful quaver in his voice.

He had hoped that getting what she wanted would put Cathy in a better mood. No such luck. "I told you we should have taken a train," she said.

"I might remind you that the only reason we're in this Jeep is because you threw a hissy fit. I know it's too much to ask for you to be grateful—I don't expect it—but isn't it pressing your luck to insult the mode of transportation?"

She huffed out a breath. "Well! If you can't stand a little criticism, you might consider getting yourself something more substantial to drive around in than this sardine can."

He rolled his eyes. "A person would think you'd never spent an uncomfortable moment in your life."

"For your information, I was eighteen before I even lived in a house with air conditioning," she said quickly. "And until I was ten, I slept in a room with four other girls, only one of whom was my sister. And as for vehicles—"

He cut her off. "I get the picture. You walked three miles to school every day in five-foot snow drifts. Catherine Seymour, long-suffering yuppie."

"I was christened Blossom," she said proudly, as if living for any amount of time with that name was a badge of honor.

And maybe it was. Hale tore his gaze from the road to stare at her in amazement. *"Blossom?"*

"Actually, my full name was Blossom Drop Seymour, but I dropped the Drop early on." She shrugged. "I suppose you could say it was a character-building experience."

She was a character, all right! He studied the silhouette of her profile, feeling his temper die down a little for the first time in the hour they'd been in the Jeep. Really, he hadn't been mad with her at all, but his own reaction to her. He was too attracted to her for his own good. The woman was practically his brother's wife.

"So how did you come by the name Cathy?" he couldn't help asking.

"When I was eighteen and left home, I studied my high school album and picked the most common name from my graduating class." She shrugged. "There was actually a tie between Cathy and Lisa, but three out of the eight varsity cheerleaders were Cathy. That gave Cathy the edge."

It must have been hard for a kid to get over disliking her identity that much. "And I thought I had it bad…"

"What was your problem?" Cathy asked.

He smiled. "I had no problems."

"And…?"

"That was it," Hale explained. He knew it sounded odd. "Everything I wanted was handed to me on a silver platter. My father wouldn't allow anything to stand in my way. If a teacher wanted to discipline me, he would make sure I got off. If I didn't make a team, he would ensure I got on. Dad's one of those micromanaging parents."

Her lips twisted wryly. "So you grew up craving to be a man of the people, with real-life ordinary problems," she guessed with embarrassing accuracy. "How noble!"

It *was* a little silly…not that he enjoyed hearing his adolescent angst trivialized. "I don't see how that's any more chowderheaded than your fanatical craving for normalcy, Harriet."

"Fanatical!" she sputtered, bristling. "Just because I want my life to have some structure."

"Answer me this. If your early family life was so traumatic and messed up that you've been running from it all your life, why on earth are you so set on marrying Bob, moving to the burbs, and starting another family?"

She arched a haughty brow at him. "That's a cynical question."

"Why?" Hale asked. "Aren't you worried you'll just have another mess on your hands?"

"Of course not!" she retorted. "The family Bob and I have will be entirely different than the one I grew up in."

"How?"

"In every way. I intend to do things right." She lifted her chin another notch. "When *my* children grow up, they'll thank me for doing such an excellent job."

Hale chuckled.

She glared at him. "What?"

"I wouldn't bank on that." He glanced over at her, trying not to notice how cute and upturned her nose was, or how perfectly shaped her profile. She had a glitter in her eyes and a set to her jaw that made him doubt her characterization of herself. Could a woman who would run into Manhattan traffic and bravely punch a kidnapper holding a gun on her really be happy standing behind a white picket fence for the rest of her life?

"Perfect, eternally grateful children aside," he couldn't help asking, "do you really think Bob and this marriage are going to give you everything you crave?"

She squared her shoulders and looked straight ahead. "Yes."

"I don't believe that for a second, and what's more, I don't think you believe it yourself."

"One day's kidnapping doesn't make you an expert on me."

Hale grinned. He did know one thing. He wasn't the only one who had been ready to betray his brother for a kiss back there on that futon. "I bet you're not half as sure of your marriage as you pretend you are."

"That's absurd! Aren't we driving to see Bob right this minute because I couldn't stand to spend one night away from him?"

He slanted a skeptical glance at her. "Or maybe you just didn't *trust* yourself to spend a night away from him..."

She didn't reply, but her chin thrust forward stubbornly, and in the headlights from the oncoming traffic he could have sworn he detected a dark blush coloring her cheeks.

"Don't worry, Harriet," he said. "I'm no nitwit. I know the score. You've been dreaming about marrying your stable Ozzie for so long that you can't envision any other life.''

Her head snapped around. ''That's so arrogant! Just because I'm not interested in you, a man who can't even dress himself...''

Hale laughed. He'd been wondering why she'd been staring at him so oddly. ''I suppose Bob dresses like something out of *GQ*.''

''Well, he usually manages to put something together that matches.''

''I like to be comfortable.''

She sniffed and lectured primly, ''It takes very little extra effort to find separates that complement each other. A pair of khaki shorts, for example, would go fine with your... T-shirt collection.''

He snorted. ''Lady, you're a hoot.''

''I don't see what's so funny about having good taste.''

''Taste is *subjective*,'' he reminded her. ''You're not the last word, you know.''

''The majority of people think that way.''

''Oh, right, I forgot. You're the one who does everything by majority vote, including naming yourself.''

''And you're the one who feels sorry for yourself because you were born with a silver spoon in your mouth!''

They spent the next half hour stewing in stubborn silence. What was the matter with him? Lord, he would be happy to wash his hands of this mess.

He should have known it was a mistake to get involved in a family matter. That was the whole trouble with families. They churned up so many feelings it was best not to deal with. His father, for instance. Just hearing the old man's voice had made him feel the disappointment and guilt he'd felt for almost a decade for letting the old man down. And for what? He'd committed the crime of wanting to become a cop and live a normal life on his own. Something that thousands of kids in America did every year without sending their families into an uproar. But not a Delaney. Oh, no!

And now there was this business with Bob. Bob, who he had no gripe with whatsoever. Oh, sure, it had been years since he had actually been *close* to his brother, but they weren't antagonistic. Yet the minute he had anything to do with Bob, he had to go and stir up bad feelings by kidnapping his fiancée…and worse, developing some sort of thing for her.

As they neared home, he found himself growing even more annoyed. Lord, he didn't want to see his father—especially on his own turf! When Kevin Delaney had proposed the kidnapping scheme, it had been in a coffee shop in midtown Manhattan. Neutral territory. Now Hale would be in the lion's den.

And Cathy. What was going to happen with her? Did she just expect him to drop her off? He scratched his stubbly jaw and threw a glance at her. "We'll be there soon."

She grunted acknowledgment.

"I expect once you see Bob, my part in this will be over," he told her. "I'll be leaving first thing in the morning."

She was silent and sat clutching her hands in her lap, one hand twisting the diamond ring on her left hand.

Damn it! He didn't actually expect her to be brokenhearted. But if she couldn't say anything nice, couldn't she at least say something snippety, words that would leave him feeling animosity toward her, instead of wishing that he'd actually kissed her when he'd had the opportunity…

"Tell me," he said, unable to resist provoking her once more. "In this neat, ordered life with Bob that you're envisioning, have you set aside a little compartment for passion?''

Her head whipped around, her mouth an *O* of surprise. "That's none of your business!"

"I was just curious," he said. "Bob is my brother, after all. I would hate to think that he's fallen prey to some kind of gold digger."

"You know that's not what I am!"

He chuckled. "Yet in all our discussions, I've never heard you mention any kind of overriding passion you have for Bob..."

Her jaw clamped shut.

"I would hate to think my brother is about to marry someone who won't be able to make him happy in *all* aspects of marriage."

She glared at him. "For your information, I appreciate everything about Bob's personality—"

"I know, he's a real pillar of virtue," Hale said, stopping the Jeep at the gates of the Delaney estate and rolling down the window to enter a pass number to open them. "But do you have the hots for him?"

"Hots?" Cathy trumpeted. "We're not adolescents. Bob and I are *beyond* the hots."

"Hmm," Hale muttered as they drove up the winding pathway to the house. "Or maybe you just breezed right over that stage?"

She sent him a withering glance. "Bob and I are about to be married. Naturally, we feel deeply for each other."

He couldn't help noticing that she refused to bandy about words like *love* and *passion*. Not very bridelike of her, he realized with undue interest. "Tell me, Harriet, when you envision this perfect television married life of yours, do you imagine the twin bed setup that Lucy and Ricky Ricardo had, or does the camera simply fade to black at the bedroom door?''

''I don't think about bedrooms at all!'' she exclaimed. Then, when he laughed, her expression turned to mortification. She faced forward again and crossed her arms stubbornly. ''I refuse to discuss this with you!''

He smiled. ''Okay, Harriet.'' At least she hadn't pretended that she and Bob had some grand passion going.

His lips turned down in a scowl. On second thought, why the hell couldn't she have told him that she and Bob *did* have a grand passion going? Now he would have to spend the next few weeks thinking about beautiful Cathy, trapping herself in a passionless marriage. Would it have killed her to have lied?

''Well, here we are,'' he said rather grimly, pulling up in the well-lit drive in front of the house. His tone could only contain a hint of the dread he felt at the prospect of crossing the threshold he'd been barred from for so long. ''Home sweet mansion.''

If ''quickest exit from a Jeep'' had been an Olympic sport, Cathy would have been the gold medalist. She stood outside the vehicle and let out a low whistle as she gaped at the mansion's impressive brick edifice. ''Mercy! How many people live here?''

''Just my father and thirteen servants. A cozy setup.'' They walked toward the front door, but before either had reached the bottom step of the porch, a window opened above them.

''Cathy!''

Cathy stopped, her eyes wide. She skipped several steps backward and looked up to the second story, where Bob hung out the window, waving at them. Cathy hopped up and down and waved back. ''Bob!''

''Cathy!''

"Bob!"

Hale smirked. "You two do a touching reunion."

Cathy tossed a glare at him, then turned her attention back to her fiancé. "Bob, are you all right?"

Bob pushed his glasses up the bridge of his nose, but they quickly slid back down. "Father locked me in my room!"

Cathy stood with her hands on her hips. "He had me kidnapped!"

"What are you doing here, Cathy? You shouldn't—"

Before Bob could finish his sentence, the front door was thrown open and Kevin Delaney stood glowering in front of them, arms akimbo. "What the blazes is going on here!" he roared.

At the sound of the bellowing baritone, Bob disappeared, the window above them slammed closed, and Cathy looked anxiously at the man in the doorway. The *tiny* man in the doorway.

Hale smiled at her startled reaction. Kevin Delaney was a regular Irish Napoleon. At five-foot-four, he looked more like a bearded leprechaun than a brewing magnate, but what he lacked in physical stature he more than compensated for in lung power. And one icy stare from those blue eyes could quell anyone.

Cathy glanced nervously at Hale.

He grinned. "Cathy Seymour, meet your future dad-in-law."

Hale's father stomped down three steps. "Oh, so you're Bob's fiancée, are you?" he demanded by way of greeting in a gruff voice that still held a trace of a brogue. "Thinkin' you're going to pull a Rapunzel rescue on your loverboy?"

Cathy blinked.

Hale laughed. "He's very pleased to meet you," he translated erroneously.

"And you!" Kevin brayed, turning those blue eyes and his wrath on his oldest and no doubt most disappointing son. "What're you doing here!"

Hale shrugged, knowing that nonchalance was the best way to handle his father—and drive his temper over the edge. He was thirty-four years old, but his father still brought out the rebellious teenager in him. "The lady wanted to see Bob."

His father's face turned a brilliant shade of burgundy. "For God's sake, man, you're supposed to be a policeman! Are you tellin' me you can't keep a girl in custody for a single day?"

"I beg your pardon!" Cathy said, stepping forward boldly. She planted her fists on her hips, mirroring Kevin's stubborn stance. "First of all, I am *not* a girl! Secondly, you can't treat people like this, kidnapping them and locking them in their rooms! You're nothing but a—a—a...dictator!"

"Weeeell!" Kevin cackled. "Bob didn't tell me he'd got himself a spunky girl!"

"Dad..."

Cathy looked as if she might explode. She stood toe-to-toe with his father, glaring down at him warningly. "I will not tolerate this type of treatment for one more moment! I demand to see Bob."

"Bob's been sent to his room till he's ready to confess."

"Bob is innocent!"

"Then he won't mind tellin' me where the money went," Kevin insisted.

Cathy rolled her eyes. "This is ridiculous. I refuse to discuss this one more minute—I'm taking Bob and we're going back to Manhattan!" Determined to storm the fortress, she put her hands to her sides and marched past Kevin.

Hale's father lifted one hand imperiously and snapped his fingers. "Swithin! Oliver!"

In answer to his call, two men appeared—the butler and gardener, in their robes and slippers. Even Swithin, who had a dapper, lithe frame and a head of hair he greased back apparently even at night, failed to look dignified in his nightclothes. Kevin pointed at Cathy, who was just making her way through the foyer and was headed toward the staircase. "Escort our guest to the Monet bedroom!"

Cathy turned just in time to see the faces of the two men who were clamping their hands down on her arms.

"And make sure she stays there till morning!"

Cathy blinked in astonishment. "You're going to lock me in?"

Kevin bobbed up and down on the balls of his feet and gloated, "Succeeding where my knuckleheaded offspring failed!" He let out a cackle that sounded half triumphant, half sneering, as he slanted a gleeful look at Hale. "Policeman, no less!"

He seemed to think that holding someone unlawfully was something a policeman should be able to do in his sleep.

As she was being dragged upstairs by the berobed goons, Cathy's astonished, angry, pleading gaze alit on Hale. "This is positively medieval! Aren't you going to say anything?"

They could have stayed in Brooklyn, but she had insisted... Hale, knowing instinctively that's not what she wanted to hear, sent her a little wave instead. "Welcome to the family."

5

"THIS IS OUTRAGEOUS!" Cathy cried, flinging her arms out, diva-fashion. But who was she yelling at? Nobody could hear her. She wasn't even certain where in the gargantuan house she was.

She sighed, sinking down onto the loud floral comforter that covered the queen-size bed. She'd craved tasteful decor all day, and now she'd gotten it in spades. Flowery chintz linens were complemented by stripes in the drapes and on a Queen Anne chair in the corner. Most of all, with the uplit gilt frame containing what appeared to be a genuine Monet painting of haystacks gracing one wall, the room was one in which Martha Stewart herself would be content to catch a few z's. Unfortunately, Cathy wasn't sleepy. She was too busy seething.

How had she done it? Unwittingly, she seemed to have finally found a family nuttier than her own! When Hale had talked about his father, she had pictured a mild eccentric with frosty manners. She hadn't expected a bad-tempered, bearded little tyrant who thought she deserved to be hauled off like a criminal just for coming to the rescue of her wrongly imprisoned fiancé. Because that's what this place was, she decided—a prison. San Quentin meets Laura Ashley. No wonder both Bob and Hale had wanted to escape and never look back. Kevin Delaney treated his grown children as if they were still toddlers; no telling how he'd behaved toward them when they actually were underage.

That pint-sized control freak was just lucky his sons had turned out as well as they had, and not turned to...

Crime? *Oh, Bob!*

Not that she for one single second believed Bob Delaney capable of doing anything illegal...under normal circumstances. But nothing about this house seemed normal. And face it, after one meeting with Herr Delaney, Sr., even she would be perfectly happy to do him injury—financial or otherwise. She wasn't letting Hale off the hook, either. He should have warned her about what she was getting herself into, but instead, he had wasted most of the long drive to Connecticut taunting her about having *the hots*—she hadn't heard that one since graduating from New Moon Montessori!

She flopped full back against the pillows and felt the blood gallop through her veins. Thank heavens it had been dark inside that jalopy—she was certain her face had been lobster red. For the truth was, she and Bob had never had much of a sex life. The timing had never worked out right. At first, Bob had wanted to sleep with her, but she had feared things were moving too fast. Then, after she'd rebuffed his initial advance, Bob had never worked up the courage to press her on the issue again.

So their lack of actual sex had simply been a little communication problem. Once they were married, everything would be fine. She was sure of it. The honeymoon change to the romantic island paradise had seemed like an omen. Besides, Bob wouldn't have agreed to marry her if he *didn't* feel some passion. Would he?

She could just imagine how smug with satisfaction Hale would be if he discovered that the seeds of doubt he'd planted were finding fertile ground in her weary mind! She hoped she never laid eyes on that man again. He had no right kidnapping her and asking her personal questions and ogling her with those gorgeous blue eyes of his...

Her lids popped open and she felt her pulse leap out of the starting gate. Good Lord! Did she have *the hots* for the wrong brother? She bolted upright. Surely her confused feelings were merely a natural extension of normal wedding-day jitters. She couldn't actually *want* Hale Delaney— her kidnapper—especially not on the very day she was to marry his far-more-desirable brother. And Bob *was* the more desirable of the two...as a mate for life.

And yet, when she shut her eyes and tried to calm down, it was Hale's face she saw, it was Hale she dreamed about kissing. She tried to concentrate on Bob. What had he wanted to say when they'd been interrupted by his father? She had to find out.

But how? How would she ever escape her floral prison and find Bob? She glanced dismissively at the door. It was locked, of that she was certain. She had spent a full ten minutes pounding on it. The bathroom had no door. The closet had no door. Which left the window.

She got up and padded to the large window seat and looked out. She was on the second floor—but it appeared to be at least twenty feet to the gravel below. Enough distance to break a few dozen bones, and even her neck if she happened to fall exactly the wrong way. And given her track record so far, if she fell, it was bound to be in exactly the wrong way.

The gods were with her in one sense: the window was nestled against a ledge perhaps eight or nine inches wide, which extended into the darkness as far as she could see with her face smashed against the window pane. She flipped the lock on the window and pulled up the sash. She was still wearing her wedding suit, and the pumps that she had dyed to match so perfectly, though comfortable, were definitely not mountain goat attire. However, her now scuffed wedding shoes would be more useful than her own callusless feet.

Once she had picked her way ten harrowing feet across the ledge, however, she began to rethink her hasty plan. She had no idea where Bob's room was. He could be in the very next room or clear on the other side of the house! She took a deep breath, trying to push that last possibility out of her mind, and hazarded a look down. The dizzying sight made her groan. She was directly above a line of pointy-leafed holly bushes.

Sweat seemed to pop from every pore in her body—including her now slippery fingertips, which were already having trouble gripping the mortar cracks between the old bricks. Cathy took another breath and began to sidle along more quickly. She reached the next window and peered through the glass, nearly shouting with relief when she saw a man's sleeping form beneath a double wedding ring quilt. He was too large to be Kevin—thank heavens! And, to her joy, she spotted Bob's glasses next to an old milk jug with a flower arrangement on a bedside table.

When she tugged on the sash, half expecting it to be locked, it flew open so easily the sudden movement nearly knocked her backward. She wobbled precariously, losing a shoe in the battle for balance, then just managed to pitch forward and fall through the window to the hardwood floors below with a *thud*. Bob, who had been snoring regularly, flopped over with an annoyed groan.

Dear Bob! How she'd missed him! She crawled across the bedroom floor, crept into bed under the covers, and slid up next to her fiancé. He felt warm and welcoming, and she flattened herself against him, spoon style. Doing so gave her a jolt of surprise. Bob wearing only boxer shorts

felt different than he usually did under layers of clothes—
more muscular and solidly male.

"Hey, puddin' buns," she purred, dredging up a jokey
endearment from their early courtship...before that first re-
buff. She enjoyed brushing her fingers along the hairs of
his muscular arms. "Guess who?"

His breathing stilled, but he didn't respond.

She'd surprised him. Pleased, she snuggled closer and
cooed, "I know you're awaaaake." She nuzzled the back
of his head. His very...*hairy*...head.

Cathy frowned. Bob's bald spot couldn't have reversed
itself in a single day, could it? Just as her heart stopped
beating, the warm body next to her turned over, and Cathy
found herself staring into a maddeningly familiar pair of
blue eyes.

Hale's eyebrows lifted in wry speculation. *"Puddin'
buns?"*

Cathy's face flamed, and her hand drew away from his
sexy, muscular arm as if recoiling from touching a slimy
slug. "What are *you* doing here?"

"I was sleeping. What were *you* doing?"

"I thought you were Bob! You snore just like him!"

He looked offended. "I do not snore."

In no mood to bicker over what was apparently a genetic
Delaney trait, Cathy asked impatiently, "And what are you
doing with Bob's glasses?" She nodded toward the wire-
rimmed frames on the bedside table.

"Those are mine. I use them to read." A smile hitched
up his lips, causing his dimple to spring to life. "Do you
really call him puddin' buns?"

"Never mind!"

Hale stared at the open window, then back at Cathy.
"How did you get in here?"

"I crawled along the ledge."

He narrowed his eyes in dismay and sat straight up. The quilt dropped around his hips as he grabbed Cathy by the shoulders. "Are you insane?"

She practically howled at the taunt. "*Insane?* You tell me! Your family sets a new threshold for the use of that term!"

"I warned you."

She shook her head. "You *didn't* warn me that your father would clap me in irons the minute I arrived on his doorstep."

"Apparently he should have taken even more precautions! Are you so bent on getting your way that you would risk your neck?"

She lifted her chin stubbornly. "I came here to see Bob."

"You could have killed yourself!"

"Well, I didn't. And now I would appreciate it if you would unhand me and take me to your brother's room."

He watched her for a moment, seeming to realize for the first time that he was touching her. But as the realization soaked in, he didn't let her go. Instead, he looked into her eyes for her own reaction. She bridled uncomfortably under his gaze, especially now that she remembered she was in bed with a man, not her fiancé, who was wearing nothing more than a pair of boxer shorts. Her own gaze, unfortunately, was level with his chest, which, close up, was stunning. Great pecs, a light dusting of hair. She felt heat instinctively build inside her and winced. How could she have been so foolish as to creep into bed with the wrong brother!

"Are you *sure* you thought I was Bob?" Hale rasped.

"Of course!" Her jaw dropped. "Are you insinuating that I actually *wanted* to crawl into bed with you?"

He chuckled. "Maybe not consciously, but…"

Her sister would have a field day with that one. "Don't

be absurd! Even my subconscious has more sense than that."

His grin sent sensual reverberations right down to the tips of her toes. "Don't be upset, Harriet. You have to admit, we fit pretty well together."

They sure did... And what's more, her skin felt like it was on fire where he was touching her. Hale was so powerful, so magnetic, that it seemed impossible to look away from him, especially when she could feel his searching gaze pinned on her. *The hots?* She felt positively feverish, and suddenly, in the silence of the bedroom, with the few inches of air crackling between them, she knew instinctively what was about to happen and had not the slightest inclination to prevent it.

He tightened his grip on her shoulders ever so slightly, then bent down and touched his mouth against hers lightly, as if testing. And if it was a test, Hale passed with flying colors. At the mere press of his warm lips against hers, she shivered with pleasure and leaned into him, wanting more. Her arms twined around his torso, playing across his bare, muscled back. His skin flinched with pleasure beneath her fingertips. And all the while, he kept up a tantalizing mating dance with their mouths, engaging her in a tongue tango with its own primordial-feeling rhythm.

It was a kiss as she'd never experienced a kiss. Deeper, more sensual than she'd imagined the mere touch of skin against skin could be. Rational thought eluded her for a moment, giving way to the irresistible urge to taste his mouth a few seconds more, to feel his arms move up and down her arms, caressing her, and to see how close she could sidle up against his chest without actually climbing on top of him. Her whole body quivered with need.

For half a day she'd been thinking about resisting this temptation, and now that the dam had broken, she was in no hurry to have it end...especially when one of those hands of his moved down to her hip and started doing some more serious exploring, causing heat lightning to shoot through every nerve ending in her body. The mere touch of his hand against her thigh made her moan with pleasure... She hadn't felt this uninhibited in years. Not since that weekend, since...

Skippy!

She dragged her mouth away from Hale's and slapped her palms against her fiery cheeks. "Oh, dear heavens!"

Hale's hands were once again braced against her shoulders—this time she feared they were all that was holding her upright. "Cathy, what's wrong?"

He had to ask? Everything! She was so appalled with herself, she couldn't speak. How could she have let herself get so carried away?

He leaned close to her, forcing her gaze to meet his. "You can't deny now that we're physically compatible."

Her face reddened and she lifted her chin, maintaining what dignity she could. "A relationship requires more than animal attraction. There needs to be a meeting of minds, too."

Hale chuckled. "I didn't hear you calling Bob puddin' brains."

She planted her hands on her hips. "Would you please just drop the puddin' bit? This is serious—it's my wedding day, and I'm in bed with a naked man I met ten hours ago!"

"Think of it this way. You didn't make a terrible mistake by marrying the wrong man."

Cathy stiffened so much that she thought her bones might snap. "Mistake?" she asked. "The only mistake I made was just now."

"You still intend to get married?" He looked confounded. "To Bob?"

"Of course!"

He shook his head. "I don't believe it. Why...?"

Who could blame him for being confused? Her behavior was erratic, to say the least. She'd had no business crawling into his bed and kissing him like that. And he was Bob's brother! Naturally, he might be worried his brother might be about to marry some kind of flake. He deserved an explanation.

She took a deep breath. "You would understand if you knew about the other time."

That caught his interest. "The other time?"

She dropped her voice, realizing she had no choice but to reveal what had been her deepest darkest secret. "I want you to know, Hale, I've never told anyone about Skippy."

Hale squinted. *"Skippy?"*

She nodded. "Skippy Dewhurst," she said, feeling miserable as she voiced the dreaded name. "You see, I was engaged once before, to my college sweetheart. It was right after we graduated. We were going to have a quiet little ceremony, then settle down where his folks lived, in Richmond."

"And your fiancé was named Skippy?"

She shook her head. "No—Skippy was his best friend, his fraternity brother. Sigma Chi. Only he was a little different...a little wilder than most college boys. And more artistic. He played guitar, acoustic guitar."

Hale nodded, but she had the sinking feeling he was hiding a smile. "He was a folk singer?"

Oh, this was all so terrible to have to admit! "Yes, that was what they called him—the frat folk singer. He was even going to sing old Bread songs at my wedding. And then, the night before the ceremony, Mr. Folk Song and I had a little too much to drink, and before I knew it..."

Hale nodded. "You woke up in bed with Skippy."

She shuddered at the memory. "In Mexico. It was terrible! I'd run off with my fiancé's best friend on the day of my wedding—*me!* After spending four years of college trying to grow away from all that Seymour flakiness, I blew it!"

"At least you didn't marry the guy you didn't love," Hale pointed out.

"But that's the worst part of all," Cathy admitted sadly. "I wasn't in love with Skippy, either. And he, when I suggested we stay together for a while, just laughed. He actually left me alone in Tijuana that very day!"

Hale shook his head. "So you think I'm like this Skippy character."

"Not exactly." Hale was worse. Much worse. Because she was so much more attracted to him. "Can't you see?" she asked him. "I must have something terribly wrong with me! All my life I've just wanted to settle down and be happy and normal, but whenever I get close to my goal, something inside me snaps! But I can't let that happen this time. You won't tell Bob, will you?"

"No..." He looked at her with dazzling, perplexed blue eyes. "So you think that kiss we just shared is something you can just walk away from?"

Could she? "It was just a kiss," she said. Just a one-time, devastating, soul-searing kiss.

Hale's lips turned down sourly.

"I *have* to marry Bob," she said emphatically. "The life we'd planned together means everything to me. We were going to move to Long Island. I'd have a real house for the first time in my life, with neighbors..."

Hale shook his head. "You're hopeless, you know that?"

Cathy caught a captivating peek at his muscled thighs and washboard abs before he reached down and pulled his shorts over his boxers. He seemed almost angry at her. "Why, because I want to live my life as planned?"

"It's not like I'm trying to keep the two of you apart," he muttered. "I was probably still half asleep when I kissed you."

Cathy tried not to feel stung by his words—and to keep her gaze away from his lips. If he could kiss like that while half asleep, just think what a few cups of coffee would do for him!

"*I* was the one who dragged you all the way out here in the first place," he reminded her. "I'm sick to death of the whole business."

"Well…good," Cathy said, licking her lips as she watched him searching the dark floor for his T-shirt. "The sooner we get this matter straightened out, the better." And the sooner she got herself away from Hale, the better.

Through the opened windows came the sound of a car coming up the drive. Cathy looked questioningly at Hale.

"It's probably the chauffeur, Tony," he explained, pulling his shirt over his head. "Tony has always had a weakness for late-night card games."

Cathy nodded. "Maybe he can take Bob and me back to town."

"Back to Manhattan?" Hale asked. *"Tonight?"*

"You don't expect us to stay here another moment, do you?"

Apparently, he had. "I can take you back," he offered.

"I would prefer—"

Her words were cut off by voices and footsteps running down the hallway. It sounded like a SWAT team. Several people barreled past Hale's room, then returned a few moments later. Suddenly, the door was thrown open and four men burst through.

One was Kevin Delaney. Next to him was Swithin, the butler, still in a bathrobe. Behind them were two policemen.

"All right!" one of the officers shouted, pushing past Kevin and Swithin and rushing toward Cathy. She recoiled instinctively but soon found herself in an iron grip. Hale's. He pulled her just out of the cop's reach.

"Put your hands up, lady."

Despite Hale's clutch on her, Cathy's hands went up automatically, but at the same time she uttered an indignant, "What is the meaning of this?"

Kevin turned to Hale, practically giving him a nudge and a wink. "The night watchman saw *this intruder* crawling across the window ledge."

"She must have entered here, sir," the other cop who was standing by the window said, giving his official stamp to the patently obvious. Then he moved across the room and snapped a handcuff around one of Cathy's wrists.

At the feel of cold steel against her skin, Cathy jumped. "Wait a second!" she said, beginning to panic. "You've got this all wrong, Officer. *I'm* the victim here."

"Right," the cop scoffed. "You're under arrest for breaking and entering, lady."

"But that's absurd! I'm being held hostage here—and so is Bob Delaney."

The cop frowned. "Lady, Bob Delaney is this man's son."

Did all officers of the law have the infuriating habit of addressing women as "lady" and saying it with such a sneer? "Ask Bob! He'll tell you the truth! We've both been kidnapped."

To her fury, Kevin Delaney shook his head in mock pity.

She turned to Hale, who let go of her arm and studied her inscrutably. What was the matter? Wasn't he going to help her?

"You have to believe me," Cathy urged the policemen. "Bob is my fiancé. That's why I'm here—to rescue him."

Kevin bounced on the balls of his feet, explaining, "It's like this every time. The woman thinks she's Bob's fiancé!"

"I *am* Bob's fiancé!"

"Then what are you doing in the brother's room?" the cop with the cuffs asked.

Cathy's face reddened as her mind happily replayed their searing kiss. "It was a mistake. I didn't know which room was Bob's…"

The cops exchanged dubious glances and Cathy knew she was sunk. Kevin Delaney had succeeded in making her look as if she were a major league wacko.

"Look, *I'm* the sane one here, *I'm* the law abider." She nodded at Kevin and Hale, the traitor, who just five minutes ago had said he'd wanted the matter cleared up! "These two are the ones you should be hauling off to the hoosegow!"

Cop Number One, dismissing her advice, turned to Kevin Delaney and explained matter-of-factly, "It's like what happened to Letterman. These women get so obsessed they'll stop at nothing."

Cathy huffed in indignation and shot an angry glance at Hale. "Why don't you tell them the truth!"

After staring at her sympathetically for a moment, Hale turned to the policemen. "She's obviously crazy." At Cathy's shriek of dismay he added, "But harmless," then turned to his father. "I don't think we need to press charges, do you, Dad? As long as she goes back to where she came from."

"Well..." Kevin Delaney rubbed his white beard, considering the matter. "If we could be sure she was gone..."

Officer Number Two eyed her sternly. "Where do you come from, lady?"

"Manhattan!" she said, red with ire.

Officer Number One nodded. "We'll take care of this for you, Mr. Delaney. You won't be troubled with this one again any time soon."

Kevin Delaney nodded. "I appreciate all your help." Then he squinted at Cathy. "Such brazen behavior! You should be ashamed of yourself, young lass!"

"You haven't seen the last of me!" Cathy vowed angrily as she was dragged from the room, limping on one pump. One glance down at her wedding suit, battle scarred from the wedding day from hell, was enough to let her know why it was so easy for the cops to believe she was a crazy woman. It was torn, snagged and smudged. Her hose were so riddled with ladders that there was barely any nylon showing. She *looked* like a nutcase. God knows, she was even beginning to feel like one.

How could this have happened to her? She'd always been so careful to avoid embarrassing situations—and not to look conspicuous. She shot a parting, withering glance at Hale. Why was he suddenly taking his father's side? She felt abandoned, betrayed and mad as hell.

As she was led out the front door of the mansion she barked, "I want my other shoe!"

The cop fetched the pump, which had landed near a holly bush.

"Where are you taking me?" she asked as they put her in the back of the patrol car. "To the station?"

Cop Number One chortled as he got behind the wheel. "The station, sure." Her heart sank. "The Amtrak station," he clarified. "Mr. Delaney was generous enough to not press charges and offer you a one-way ticket back to Manhattan. But the next time we find you creeping around harassing innocent people, you won't be so lucky.''

"Yeah." His counterpart swung back to glare at her menacingly as the car pulled out the Delaney mansion's gates. "The State of Connecticut has a place for lunatics.''

Cathy laughed out loud at his threat. "I know. I've just been there!''

The cops exchanged glances and shook their heads pityingly.

As soon as the cops had hauled Cathy away, Hale took a deep breath and turned to his father. "You know, Dad, you can't treat people like this forever and expect to get away with it." The warning was pointless, he knew, but still he felt compelled to say it.

His father cackled in delight, his eyes still twinkling from the sight of Cathy being dragged off in cuffs by the boys in blue. "Didn't she look a sight?" he asked. "Ha! Where do you think that brother of yours dredged up such an unpleasant creature?''

Hale blinked in surprise. To him, the wonder had been that Bob had managed to find himself such a dish! "Didn't you like her at all?''

"Like her?" His father's gray eyebrows shot up almost to his hairline. "That snippy thing? That harpy? Why, that girl didn't have a civil word to say to me!''

"You weren't exactly the soul of hospitality," Hale reminded him.

Kevin looked genuinely shocked. "I gave her the Monet bedroom. Nicest room in the house! Your mother decorated it!''

And it hadn't been changed in over twenty years. Nothing in this house ever changed.

Kevin's eyes zeroed in on Hale suspiciously. "Don't tell me *you* like that woman, that what's-her-name?"

"Cathy." Hale could feel his jaw working.

His father let out another cackle. "Oh-ho!" he trilled. "A little brotherly rivalry still going on, I see..."

His father always liked to cook up hard feelings between him and Bob. "I've never been jealous of Bob." *Not until now...* Hale felt his face go red. He just wanted to drop the subject. "I've tried to help you, Dad, but at some point—"

His father paced anxiously. "At some point Bob has to break down and tell me the truth. Maybe now that he knows that fiancée of his won't be riding to his rescue, he'll come around."

Hale felt torn between two opposing but equally nutty points of view. The sympathy he felt for his father, despite every lousy thing he'd done, surprised him. Ever since Bob and Hale's mother had died when they were still little boys, it seemed Kevin Delaney could express emotion only through bullying—even if it meant kidnapping and, yes, cutting people out of his will. He showed his love through manipulation. Yet Hale also felt a loyalty to Cathy that he hadn't expected. She hadn't asked for any of this.

Yes, she had screwed-up ideas about what life should be like. And certainly, he thought she was wrongheaded to want to run back to Bob's arms when she'd fit so well in his own. But she had spelled out her wedding plans clearly from the very beginning, and he'd known that he didn't figure into them. Every person had a right to their dreams. Hale's father never understood the life Hale had chosen, but that didn't mean being a cop was wrong. Cathy had a right to her Ozzie and Harriet dreams. Heck, she almost made them look good, even.

While the police were there, Hale had thought returning Cathy to Manhattan was a way to rescue her. But rescue her from what? From Kevin? From Bob…or from himself? Their few minutes in bed together had been way too tempting. If it had been up to him, he wasn't certain he could have stopped. And what about Cathy? She hadn't *looked* like she wanted him to stop. He'd bought her story about Skippy What's-his-name, but could she really go through with her plan to marry Bob?

"Is that your detective face?" his father asked.

Hale looked up, suddenly realizing that he'd been lost in thought. An idea struck him. Detecting? Why not? What had happened to the Delaneys' lost millions didn't particularly interest him, but what happened to Cathy, on the other hand, was worth looking into. And, so far, he'd only heard one side of the story. Hers. *That* wasn't very good detective work.

"Maybe I'm not quite ready to wash my hands of this whole thing yet," he admitted, surprising himself. His whole life, he'd been running from family matters, but here he was, just digging himself in deeper.

His father barked out a laugh. "Can't see that you've been much of a help so far!"

"Maybe because I haven't spoken to the main person."

His father looked befuddled. "What are you talkin' about? I've told you everything I know!"

Leave it to Kevin never to see himself as a supporting player. "I meant Bob, Dad," Hale corrected him. "I think it's time I spoke with that brother of mine."

6

SQUINTING SUSPICIOUSLY at his brother, Bob pushed his glasses up his nose. "Whose side are you on?"

Cathy's, was what came to Hale's mind, but then he remembered that Cathy only wanted to prove Bob's innocence so she could rush headlong into marriage to Bob. That wasn't exactly the goal Hale was aiming for. "I'm just trying to find out the truth."

That statement made Bob look depressed. "No one believes me," he said, pacing over to his bed and collapsing on it. He was wearing a pair of starchy-looking long-sleeved paisley pajamas. Hale would have bet money that Cathy had picked them out.

"I do." Once they were out, Hale couldn't believe he'd said those words. Maybe he'd been around Cathy too long.

Bob looked at him suspiciously. "Oh, sure. That's why you're in cahoots with Dad."

"I just did this one favor for him," Hale told his brother. He lifted his shoulders and added ruefully, "I'm sorry it had to involve kidnapping your fiancée, but believe me, I'm not on his side particularly. It's just that Dad can seem so needy sometimes."

"I know," Bob said with a hint of exasperation. "Half the time I've been here he's been hounding me about the missing money, which he thinks I took, and then the other half, he's been playing gin rummy with me and trying to convince me to go to work as head of accounts of Delaney Ale!''

"Even though he thinks you've stolen from the family?''

Bob nodded. "He's even offered to start me off higher than what I make at the bank, as long as I give the money back. I've told Dad over and over that I've done nothing—he won't believe me. And he won't let me out of here. He's even instructed Swithin not to let me have access to the kitchen.'' If anything, this made Bob look even more distressed than the fact that his own father thought he was a crook. "I'd kill to make a batch of brownies. The chewy kind, with walnuts.''

Hale nodded. Bob always did have a flair for desserts. Maybe that's what gave him that special Bob look—like how the Pillsbury Doughboy might have appeared if he'd majored in accounting. "Then maybe you should tell Dad who did take the money, so he'll let you go.''

Bob's eyes bugged. "B-but...''

After eight years of police work, it became second nature to know when people were hiding something. Bob might not be lying, but there was something he didn't want others to know. "Who's Bernie Morton?'' Hale asked him.

"Bernie? What makes you mention him?''

"Cathy told me about him.''

"Cathy knows?''

"Knows what?''

Bob's jaw slammed shut. "Nothing.''

Nothing, my foot, Hale thought. "You think Bernie Morton's been funneling money from the family? When they first found the money missing, Swithin nosed around the bank, and he said one of your co-workers told him *you* were acting suspiciously. Do you think that co-worker could have been Bernie?''

Bob looked confounded. "He's my oldest friend. Didn't you ever see him around here?"

Hale shook his head. "I don't remember him."

"Maybe you'd moved out by then, but he used to come out a lot. We were college roommates, and we went to business school together."

"So would Dad remember him? And the servants?" Hale asked.

"I guess so," Bob said.

"Maybe that's why Swithin would have talked to him…"

His brother nodded. "I just can't imagine why Bernie would do something like this…"

"But nevertheless you think he did."

Bob looked miserable. "Well, I suspected. He kept acting oddly—taking secretive phone calls at work. We'd be talking and the phone would ring, and he'd answer it and then wave me out of the office. That was weird. One time he even locked the door behind me. And about two weeks ago, I came into work extra early, and I found him in my office, and my computer was on."

Hale nodded. Looks like they had their man. "What excuse did he give?"

"He said my software has a game called Solitile on it, and his doesn't." Bob shrugged. "He might have been telling the truth about that. But what really made me suspicious was that he's been acting really erratic and restless. He's been drinking too much—and a little while ago he took this spur-of-the-moment vacation to the Cayman Islands. So I was going to run down there to check things out."

"On your honeymoon," Hale guessed.

"Yeah…but I never got the opportunity."

Hale shook his head. "Why didn't you just tell Dad all

this right away? If Bernie's actually been doing all you suspect, he can't be that good a friend.''

"But what if he's innocent?" Bob asked, looking pained. "If I point the finger at him..."

That wasn't something a friend would forgive you for. And Hale knew from experience that Bob wasn't one to snitch. One time Hale had dented the fender on his father's Mercedes, and Bob had taken the blame for the damage rather than tell on Hale, who had confessed as soon as he learned that Bob had sacrificed a school field trip to the New York Stock Exchange on his behalf. If that wasn't brotherly love, he didn't know what was. The memory, and the fact that he was still willing to stand by his friends faithfully until absolutely certain they were guilty, caused Hale to feel a swell of admiration for his paisley-clad sibling.

He considered the information about Bernie Morton for a minute. "But if you suspected him, and were even willing to change your honeymoon plans because of those suspicions..."

Bob waved his hands. "It was no big deal. I didn't really want to go to Amish country anyway—that was Cathy's idea."

"But I would think you would want to throw the suspicion off yourself so you could get on with your life?"

His brother looked perplexed. "What life?"

Hale rolled his eyes. "You know, your wedding...your *honeymoon?*"

Bob shrugged. "Oh, that."

Spoken like an eager groom! Hale tilted his head. "Don't you *want* to marry Cathy?"

Bob's expression was startled and he puffed up defensively. "Of course I do!" After a tense, assessing stare from Hale, he deflated. "Sort of..."

Hale shot out of the desk chair where he'd been sitting and began to pace like a tiger in a cage. Bob, Cathy's dream man, didn't want to get married? Hale didn't like the way his heart was racing, or the difficulty he was experiencing hiding a gleeful grin. Just because Bob wasn't fingering his best friend so he could race to the altar didn't mean the wedding was off...but it did make it a little more unlikely.

Hale usually left playing devil's advocate to the lawyers, but he did feel compelled to point out, "Cathy is hell-bent on getting an 'I do' out of you."

Bob nodded miserably, ratcheting up Hale's hopes another notch. "I know. And I want to marry her, I really do. Gosh, who wouldn't?" He shrugged again. "It's just..."

Hale felt like shaking him. "Just what?"

"I just feel we're rushing things. We've only known each other three years."

"Three years is a long time, bro," Hale pointed out. "Most marriages don't last that long, these days."

"Of course, for *most* people three years would be a substantial waiting period," Bob admitted, looking uneasily at his brother. "But Cathy and I haven't had one of those fast, modern relationships."

"Oh...?" Hale asked, not quite sure what his little brother was getting at. Fast? Modern?

"You know..." Bob said, his face so red he could have doubled for a vine-ripened tomato. "Our private life hasn't exactly been something off 'Melrose Place.'"

Hale thought for a moment, at first sidetracked by the idea of Bob, a *Wall Street Week* junkie from way back, even knowing a steamy location called Melrose Place existed. But after a few seconds, the core of what Bob was trying to relay to him finally sank in. "You mean you two haven't...?"

Bob shook his head frantically in order to stop his

brother from giving voice to any of the euphemisms for sex, which Hale was more than happy to do. He was so stunned! Cathy and Bob, apparently, had been prevented from having what would surely have been the last traditional wedding night in the Western world!

Poor Bob looked like he wanted to crawl under the bed. "That's the only good thing I can think about being here. It might give us both a little room to think whether we're doing the right thing. And if I could just bribe Swithin to get the cook to whip up some decent desserts, I would be a lot happier."

He couldn't believe Bob would be craving sugar when Cathy had just been yanked out of his grasp. "Bob, what about your fiancée?"

Bob shook his head. "She doesn't like me to eat sweets."

Hale took a breath for patience. "I meant, what are you going to do about Cathy once you get out of this mess?"

Bob hesitated. "I'm not certain…"

"Don't you think you ought to be sure?" Hale asked, unable to keep an indignant swipe out of his tone.

Bob nodded. "Cathy assures me we're made for each other."

"Cathy would." She was so determined to commence her dream life in the suburbs, nothing—especially not a mere matter of incompatibility—was going to stop her from snagging Bob.

Bob grinned. "I guess you've gotten to know her. She's a little…"

"A little like a steamroller?" Hale guessed. "She's determined to get you out of here. That's why she insisted I drive her out tonight."

Bob nodded. "I saw the police dragging her off."

"That was just as well. If they hadn't, she might have

hurled herself off the roof in an escape attempt. It was getting a little dangerous keeping her in captivity.''

''Like I said...I think it's best we stay apart for a few days. That's why I'm not trying too hard to escape. Now that Dad's on to the missing money, I'm not so worried about it.'' Bob's rueful smile morphed into a frown. ''But it might be dangerous for Cathy back in Manhattan. She's likely to start poking around.''

Hale hadn't thought of that. ''At work?''

Bob nodded. ''I need to call her and tell her to stay put.''

Hale's feet were already directing him toward the door. ''I'll do better. I'll make certain she doesn't do any sleuthing.''

Bob shot him a dubious glance. ''Getting Cathy to do what you want is easier said than done. You might have to watch her.''

Hale laughed. ''I intend to. Round the clock.''

When he left his brother's room, Hale almost mowed down Swithin in the hallway. The butler jumped back, keeping the tea tray he carried on one hand expertly balanced in spite of the collision.

''Oh, Swithin!'' Hale exclaimed, surprised to see him. It was so late, and he was in such a hurry to get back to Manhattan and Cathy that he hadn't expected to run into anyone.

The butler nodded. ''I was just carrying some tea to Mr. Bob. After all the excitement, I thought a cup of tea might soothe everyone's nerves.''

''You can skip my room, I'm going back tonight,'' Hale informed him. ''From what I've been hearing, this family owes you one, Swithin.''

Swithin's dark eyes registered the compliment, but his mouth pursed in displeasure. ''A butler never expects thanks, sir.''

How anyone could be so placid would forever remain a mystery to Hale. The man was so emotionless it almost irritated him. "Nevertheless, we owe you." He thought for a moment, while Swithin, obviously growing weary of standing in the hallway with the tea, started edging toward Bob's door. Hale frowned, stopping him. "I was wondering…"

Swithin's jet black brows shot up. "Yes?"

"Dad told me you had spoken to someone at the bank about Bob. Was that someone Bernie Morton?"

Swithin thought for a moment. "Yes, I believe it was. You see, I knew him from before."

"From when Bob was in college?"

"Yes, sir. He was hard to forget—a rather ungainly looking youth, dark hair and pale, pale skin. He was all pimples and gangly limbs. He had quite a nervous, pinched look about his eyes, too."

"And now?" Hale asked.

Swithin's lips twisted wryly. "Well, his skin has cleared up a bit."

Hale guessed everything else was the same. He committed the description to memory and decided to let Swithin be on his way. Then, as he was halfway to the stairs, he stopped. "Oh, and Swithin?"

The long-suffering butler turned. "Yes, Mr. Hale?"

He nodded at the tray. "Could you find it in your heart to slip Bob a couple of cookies or something sweet?"

Sending Hale a rare smile, Swithin uncovered a slice of cake with fresh strawberries and cream. "Done, sir."

He grinned. He wanted his brother to be happy in captivity. As long as Bob, unlike himself, was in no hurry to get back to Cathy, that would suit Hale's purposes just fine.

NEVER, NEVER IN HER LIFE had Cathy expected to feel elation at seeing a member of her own family. But when Joan opened the door for her at three o'clock in the morning, Cathy exuberantly hugged her sister—spiky orange hair and all. Now that she'd met the mentally ill Delaneys, never again would she be embarrassed by the benignly flaky Seymours.

"Damn!" Joan gaped in amazement at the tattered, no-longer-tasteful, or even beige, dress that she had once scolded her sister for purchasing, declaring it too boring. "You must have had one hell of a wedding day!"

"There was no wedding." Cathy felt tears building in her eyes, and tossed herself onto her sister's leopard fun fur couch in exhaustion. She recounted her wedding day woes hour by hour, from the moment she woke up, suspecting nothing of the catastrophe about to befall her, right down to when she stumbled off the train at Penn Station and hailed a cab to take her to her sister's apartment. It felt so good to get the whole thing off her chest—to let someone else try to make sense of the chaos that had suddenly overtaken her carefully planned life.

"Let me get this straight," Joan said, thoughtfully tapping a long orange-painted nail against her chin. Cathy guessed the nails went with the hair. She gave her sister credit for attempting to match, at least. "The hunk who kidnapped you is boring Bob's brother, but the father doesn't like him, either?"

Cathy nodded, but added automatically, "Bob is *not* boring."

Joan raised an orange brow dubiously.

"He's not," Cathy insisted. This was their oldest argument. "You just have a skewed standard. You go for spidery looking men in black with names like Igor and Leonardo and Prince."

"Duke," Joan corrected tersely. "His name is Duke."

"Oh, that's right. Prince is the name of a fellow who used to be a rock star."

"He's still a rock star. He just doesn't have a name now. And for your information, Duke and I are still together. He's even got a job, driving a cab."

Cathy smiled indulgently. "Two weeks, and they're still like newlyweds."

"Oh, well, never mind *me*," Joan said in the irritated voice she always used when anyone started examining her own life with the same zeal she used on everyone else. She paced back and forth. A silk kimono fluttered loosely over her pajamas, which consisted of a pair of boxer shorts and a tight tank T-shirt. For slippers she wore a pair of green slouch socks, one of which had worked its heel down to her toe, so that most of it flopped limply as she walked. All in all, she looked pretty good for someone pulled out of bed at three in the morning to listen to wild stories of cops and kidnappings.

"You seem especially upset by this man...this Hale..."

"Of course! He was the one who kidnapped me."

"Hmmm..."

Cathy narrowed her gaze on her sister. "I know," she guessed. "You think that secretly I'm falling in love with him and out of love with Bob. You think that subconsciously I wish Bob would get convicted of embezzling and sent to the pen for twenty years."

"Even three years would be sufficient," Joan said.

"*Bob is innocent!*" Cathy cried. What would it take to make people believe her?

"Yes, yes, yes," Joan said. "Of course he is. Bob is a gem. Now about this Hale..."

"I told you, I just want to forget him."

"Of course you do," Joan shot back smartly. "That's why you pounded on my door at three in the morning to tell me all about him, from his Paul Newman eyes to the muscles in his chest.''

Maybe she *had* provided too much detail. At least she hadn't told her sister about the kiss—*that* might have thrown Joan into speculation overdrive. "I'm still just so stunned. What can I do to get Bob away from those people?''

Joan sighed and settled into an armchair. "You want my advice?''

Cathy nodded. Usually advice from her sister was something she savored about as much as an IRS audit, but she'd had a hell of a day, and she needed help.

"Do nothing,'' Joan said. She propped her elbows on the armrests of her chair and steepled her orange-tipped fingers. "Of course, I've only met one of the Delaneys, but from what you've told me tonight, my opinion on that family would be that they're all bonkers. Nutcases. Loony birds.''

"But Bob isn't crazy. He's not guilty of embezzling, either. The only thing he's guilty of is having a paranoid father and a brother who would stop at nothing to ingratiate himself to said father, including letting me be hauled off by the police like a common criminal!'' Cathy felt righteous anger building within her all over again. "I've got to do something to help him!''

"And what about this Hale person? Are you really going to forget he swept you off your feet?''

"He did nothing of the kind,'' Cathy said, sitting up. "He kidnapped me. At gunpoint. He belongs in a padded cell.''

Joan shot her a level stare. "And when are you and Bob going to attempt to tie the knot again?''

Cathy jumped off the couch in a huff. "Just as soon as I can pry him loose from his father!'' she said, looking around for her purse. She marched to the door, newly determined. If no one would believe her when she said Bob was innocent, she would just have to find evidence to prove her case. "It won't take much to clear Bob now that I'm back in New York and can really put my shoulder to the wheel."

"Be careful you don't get yourself in trouble," Joan warned.

"What do you mean?"

"I mean wheels have a tendency to spin out of control," her sister replied. "And that outfit you've got on looks like it has tire tracks on it already."

By the time Cathy flagged down a cab and reached her own home, a brownstone in which she occupied the basement floor, she was exhausted. Unfortunately, as soon as she opened the gate leading to her door, she jolted wide awake once again. She hadn't had to use her key; usually the gate was locked. Had she been so flustered about her marriage yesterday that she'd forgotten to lock it?

As she moved to push her key into the lock on her front door, it swung open to reveal her living room—in a shambles. Someone had ransacked her apartment! She stood stock-still, almost afraid to take a step forward through the muddle of clothes and books and overturned couch cushions. What a mess! Who could have—

She looked up, suddenly terrified that whoever had given her apartment this going-over was still in there. Or worse, was *watching her.* The blood drained out of her face and her heart slammed against her ribs.

Brrrrrrrr-innng!

At the unexpected noise, Cathy shot straight up in the air like a flea and landed with one foot flat on a nightgown and the other twisting on her copy of a thick paperback beach book.

Brrrrrrrr-innng!

The phone! Where was it? She hop-limped around the clutter until finally landing on the phone, knocking over the receiver. She fell to her hands and knees and, huddling behind a chair, caught her breath. "Hello?"

"Cathy? Is that you?"

"Bob!" She nearly wept with relief. "Thank heavens! Where are you?"

"I'm still in Connecticut."

"Oh, Bob, you'll never believe it. My apartment—"

He didn't let her finish. "I don't have much time, Cathy, but when you see Hale, tell him about Dexter."

"Hale!" Cathy exclaimed, amazed how the name could get her ire up even in the midst of a personal calamity. "Listen, Bob, I don't want to offend you, but I hope never to see that brother of yours again as long as I live!"

"He should be there today sometime to check on you," Bob said, heedless of her words. "Tell him if he looks into the computers at the bank, Dexter would be—"

Cathy winced as the receiver on his end apparently slipped out of his fingers and clattered against something hard, creating a minor explosion in her ear. "Bob!"

He picked it up again. "I have to go—"

"Bob, no. I need to ask you what I should do about my…"

She heard footsteps coming down the sidewalk stop outside the gate to her apartment. Oh, no! She whispered frantically into the phone. "Bob, there's someone here! I'm so afraid. My place has been—"

There was a clattering in her ear again, and then the phone went dead.

Cathy didn't know what to do. She'd lost Bob, who had been trying to tell her something important. There was a shadow in her doorway. And God knows what she'd find in her bedroom. When the shadow moved, she sank down lower against the chair, knowing it wasn't much of a camouflage, and dialed 911.

"Cathy?"

She looked up. Hale!

He peeked inside the open door, his blue eyes widening in surprise for a second, then narrowing cautiously on her. Overwhelmed by equal parts relief and confusion, Cathy slammed the receiver down. Bob had just warned her Hale would try to find her—and here he was. But what was he doing here? She hadn't wanted to see him again as long as she lived…but right this minute she felt conflicted. She jumped up, then hesitated, not certain whether or not she should go with the instinct to throw herself into his arms. The last time she'd been in those arms she hadn't felt particularly safe…

They stood awkwardly amidst the clutter for a few moments, until at last Hale cracked a smile and gestured to all the clothes strewn across the floor at their feet. "And you bragged about your housekeeping!" he exclaimed.

Cathy put her hands on her hips and glared at him. "You've got a lot of nerve marching in here and making wiseacre cracks!"

Hale was relieved. Bickering he could deal with. Coming in and finding Cathy blinking up at him, appearing as forlorn in her own apartment as she had in his, had been more than he could take. She'd had that shaken, violated look that he'd seen on burglary victims' faces for years, but seeing it on her made him feel choked. Even now as he looked into her flashing brown eyes he felt emotion hitch his chest. *Relief.* It was just relief that she was safe that clamped his heart like a vise. Anything else would be uncalled for. The woman was practically his brother's wife, even if he intended to have his say before that became an irreversible fact.

He took another step inside, nearly tripping over a blue strappy sandal lying in the small foyer. "At least I got you talking." A little venting would be good for her. He began to make his way through the apartment, though he doubted he would find an intruder. This type of job wasn't usually done at seven in the morning.

Cathy was right on his heels as he ducked into the kitchenette area and checked a broom closet. "I've got a bone to pick with you!"

A mop fell out and Cathy, who was apparently still more shaken than she cared to show, yelped. She also clamped a hand onto his arm with the circulation-inhibiting squeeze of a boa constrictor.

Gritting his teeth, he propped the mop back into place and shut the door again. "What's on your mind?"

She let go of him and folded her arms, dogging his heels as he headed toward the bedroom. "Last night!"

He flicked a grin at her. "You mean when you crawled into bed with me? That was *your* fault…"

"I meant pretending that you'd never seen me before when the cops showed. Letting them haul me off like some lunatic!"

He laughed as he checked behind the bedroom door.

"You're a toad!" she said disparagingly. Then, nibbling on her lip, she touched his arm gently and pointed to a door on the opposite wall. "The closet's over there."

Toads had their uses, apparently. There was nothing in the closet but clothes hanging and sweaters folded tidily on a set of cedar shelves. Very neat. He glanced across the room at the dresser. It, too, seemed untouched. Hale frowned. "What do you think they were looking for?"

"Why don't you call your father and ask him?"

Surprised, he pivoted. "You think my family was responsible for *this?*"

"Who else?" she asked.

"Believe me, Cathy, my father had nothing to do with this. Breaking and entering is not his style."

"As opposed to kidnapping and lying to the authorities?"

He could see where she might have jumped to the wrong conclusion. "I swear to you, this had nothing to do with my father. How long have you been here?"

"Five minutes, tops."

That would explain why she was still wearing that sad-looking wedding outfit. "And who were you talking to on the phone?"

Her mouth snapped closed. Then, after a second's thought, she replied, "No one."

He tilted his head skeptically. "I heard you speaking. You were talking to Bob, weren't you?"

She shook her head adamantly. "No."

"What did he tell you?"

"Nothing," she said.

"Then that *was* Bob on the phone, wasn't it?"

Her chin lifted stubbornly. "I'm not speaking to you."

"I don't see why not. Bob is."

She blinked in disbelief, so Hale decided to feed her some more information. "He even gave me a name for our prime suspect. Bernie Morton."

She took a moment to let the name sink in, then shook her head vehemently. "That's impossible!"

"Why?"

"Because Bernie and Bob are like brothers!" Realizing who she was talking to, she added, "Brothers who actually get along. They've been friends forever, and they're big pals at the bank. They both have a reputation of being model workers, and even have a contest going to see who can be named employee of the month most often."

"That doesn't preclude his also being embezzler of the month."

She pursed her pretty lips at him. "It would be out of character for Bernie. He can barely keep a secret. On days when the office has a surprise birthday party for someone, he skulks around all day till the big event looking like he's in agony. He would never be able to steal the amounts you're talking about."

"Bob thinks otherwise," Hale said.

"He didn't mention that to me," she said. Then, realizing what she'd just revealed, she slapped her hand over her mouth.

Hale laughed. "What *did* he have to say then?"

"Nothing!"

"C'mon, Cathy, you can tell me. You might find this hard to believe, but I'm on your side."

She cackled in disbelief. "Gee, it's great having you on my team. I guess that's why you let the police haul me away last night like some wacko."

He shook his head. "I was trying to get you away from my father."

"A likely story!" she exclaimed.

He decided it might be good politics to drop the matter for the time being. He looked back around the apartment. "So do you have any idea of what's missing from here?"

She stared almost mournfully around the room, the contents of which looked as if they had been shaken, turned upside down, and spilled on the ground. "Order," she said glumly. "That's what's missing."

Hale tried to imagine the room as it might have looked if clean. The sofa and matching chair were a neutral beige color. Naturally, with her hyperactive idea of normal, Cathy wouldn't want any loud prints that would be hard to match. There were no pillows visible, and from Cathy's words on the subject of throw pillows, he doubted he would find any beneath the piles of magazines, books and clothes.

He frowned. "Why would they have dragged your clothes into the living room?"

"I had my suitcase in here," she explained. "For the honeymoon trip."

Hale frowned as he caught sight of a navy blue one-piece bathing suit in a shiny heap at his feet. By most standards, it was a practical suit, but when he imagined it fitting snugly around Cathy's body, her body which just last night had squeezed next to his like a glove, it revealed far more of her than he was comfortable thinking about.

He cleared his throat. "Where's the suitcase?"

"On the kitchen floor," she said. "I'd left it sitting by the front door, so that on the way to the airport, I could just dash in and grab it. I didn't want to lug it to City Hall."

Hale nodded, not in the least surprised that Cathy had planned her wedding day to the last second. "We need to figure out what was in the suitcase, and what's missing from it."

Both of them began scooping up items from the floor. Hale followed Cathy's lead and stacked what he found in neat piles—shorts, knit tops, shoes, toiletries. He held up a silky wisp of a bra and smiled. "Where should this go?"

Her hand snatched the garment out of his grasp. "Are you *sure* your family had nothing to do with this?" she asked testily.

"Positive." Even Kevin Delaney wouldn't have someone toss Cathy's apartment.

"I'm not certain I—" Her next words lodged in her throat and she turned, white-faced, and riffled through the book and magazine pile.

"What is it?" Hale asked.

"The plane tickets!" she exclaimed. "I left them in my suitcase, but now they're in the bedroom, next to the telephone on the nightstand."

Hale nodded, remembering now seeing the travel agent's envelope. They went into the bedroom and inspected the two tickets to the Cayman Islands. "Are you certain you didn't leave them here?"

Cathy shook her head. "I packed them. I always put tickets in the side pocket of my carry-on bag. Always."

"So someone wanted to know where you were headed."

"Doesn't this prove Bob is innocent?" Cathy asked. "The tickets were round trip. He wouldn't have bothered with that if he'd planned to skip the country. And Bob wouldn't have broken into *my* apartment."

Hale frowned.

"You still don't believe him one hundred percent, do you?" Cathy asked.

Hale crossed his arms. "This isn't TV. Suspects just aren't crossed off a checklist."

"I know that. I'm not an imbecile."

No, she wasn't. She was smart, and funny, and loyal—what was it in him that coveted all that smartness and humor and loyalty? Why did he wish he were kissing the pout off those full lips instead of staring at her as if she were forbidden fruit?

Which is what she still was, he reminded himself. He needed to get a grip. He turned and pointed at something that had been bothering him since he'd walked in. "Okay, if you're so smart, can you tell me why you're living in a basement apartment in New York City with only one flimsy lock on the door? You need a dead bolt here."

Cathy trotted behind him and inspected her door. She

frowned at the flimsy latch that someone had easily picked. "I'll call a locksmith right now," she said decisively.

"Good. And while we're waiting for them, we can get the police over and dust the place for prints."

She looked startled. "The police? But *you're* the police."

"Sure, but I don't run around with a detective's lab in my back pocket."

"Nothing was stolen. Why make a fuss?"

He put his hands squarely on her shoulders. "Cathy, your apartment has been broken into. Breaking and entering, even without theft, is a crime."

"Maybe so, but right now I've got bigger problems."

Oh, no, Hale thought with dread. "You're not going to start playing amateur sleuth, are you?"

"Of course not!" Cathy scoffed. "I just don't want policemen crawling around my apartment. I'm exhausted. I'm still wearing my wedding clothes, I need a shower, and some sleep! Can you blame me for wanting some privacy?"

"But the person who broke in—"

"Won't be back," Cathy said, cutting him off. "Whoever it was just wanted to find out where we were going. Why would he return?"

Hale could understand her being tired. God knows, he was, too. And she obviously wasn't going to let the police search her house.

"All right," he said, giving in reluctantly. When it came to work, he was normally a by-the-book person. But nothing about this little intrigue was normal. "I know a locksmith. I'll call him and we'll clean the place up while we wait. Then you can take a shower and crash."

"Thank you," she said, dropping a sarcastic little curtsy.

He knew he sounded paternalistic, but he couldn't help

himself. "And for heaven's sake, don't go around trying to solve an embezzling scam on your own. White-collar criminals can get just as vicious as street thugs, if they're cornered."

"I'll leave the sleuthing in capable Delaney hands."

Hale hunted down the phone and directory in the debris.

"Do you want to interrogate me further, or may I start cleaning now?" Cathy asked.

As Hale punched the number for the locksmith, he looked over at a pile of incredibly sheer underwear and grinned. He shouldn't, he knew, but he couldn't help himself. Prim Cathy was an irresistible target. "Just a quick question," he said.

One of her eyebrows shot up inquisitively. "Yes?"

He nodded to the panties on the coffee table. "Do you always wear things like that, or do you save the sheer stuff for special occasions?"

7

BOB HAD MENTIONED A Dexter. He said that if Hale checked the computers at the bank, he would need Dexter. Cathy scanned the FIB's phone list for the name, but came up with nothing. She did find someone listed as D. Simonton, but discovered that the *D* stood for David. There were no Dexters at the FIB. Maybe she should have mentioned the name to Hale—but how could she be sure he was on their side? Just because he might have wheedled his way into Bob's confidence didn't mean that she should trust him, too. At least not till she'd checked some things out on her own. That's why she'd decided to go in to work the moment Hale had left her apartment and she'd had a few hours' sleep.

So far, what disturbed her even more than her lack of success in locating the mysterious Dexter was the easy way people at the bank swallowed her lie about having cancelled her honeymoon because Bob had a cold. Few coworkers knew that she and Bob had eloped, yet none of even the select few they'd told seemed surprised that she would be back at the office the afternoon after her wedding day.

They all think I'm some kind of passionless stick-in-the-mud, she realized with a jolt. *Was* she a stick-in-the-mud? Or passionless? Just because she preferred the predictability and stability of Bob over Hale, who was an unknown quantity wrapped in a handsome package?

She *did* prefer Bob, didn't she?

She leaned back in her desk chair and stared unseeingly at her monitor. She'd never felt so strange. Edgy. It seemed as if the granite solid foundation of normalcy she'd built her life upon was shifting and crumbling beneath her. Never before she met Hale had she doubted her intention to marry Bob. Now she had to force herself to remember she was an engaged woman. All she could think about was Hale, and how it had felt to be in that bed with him.

She'd been so glad to see him in her apartment that every inch of him had seemed delectable, even though he'd shown up wearing an old pair of jeans—never her favorite garment choice. And these jeans were so worn that they hugged him in all the right places, diverting her attention from the unseemly hole in the right knee. His T-shirt for the day hailed from someplace called the Old Lonesome Bar. Naturally, this obviously cherished item of clothing had *not* been tucked in.

That was just the trouble—nothing about Hale was tucked in or neat or easy to pigeonhole. He was a cop who kidnapped people. His conversation ranged from lecturing her on safety to Handel to speculating on her panties! She didn't know what to expect from him. She surely hadn't anticipated the warm concern and anger in his eyes when he'd walked in and seen her sitting in the clutter.

She looked down at her desk for a moment and attempted to focus on some real work, to test whether she could actually get her mind off Hale. Since coming to the FIB three years before, loans had been her life. Loans and Bob and her dreams. She stared now at a credit report—a solid one with no outstanding debt—and felt not an iota of interest. How could that be?

Fearing for her sanity, she closed her eyes for a moment and gave herself the ultimate test. Usually it wasn't difficult at all to conjure up the vision of the perfect house that she and Bob would buy. It was two-story, brick, on at least a half-acre, woodsy lot. Maybe they would even live in a cul-de-sac, where kids rode their bikes in the circle while moms stood in their yards swapping recipes and gardening tips. One day when she and Bob decided it was time to have kids, she would give up her life of loans and dedicate herself to becoming the kind of supermom she'd always wished she'd had.

But today when she tried to conjure her life in the suburbs, all she could think about, strangely enough, was the in-box on her desk. How many loan applications would pass through the office in the time it took her to raise two point five children? Work was already piling up after a day-long honeymoon. She loved her work. And more disturbing yet, when she tried to picture the stalwart male who would be at her side, Bob didn't pop up on her mental screen. Instead, she envisioned Hale, who grinned sexily at her in a very unsuburban way.

Her eyes flew open, and reflected in her monitor, she saw a man pass her office. Bernie Morton! Cathy snapped out of her Hale-induced funk and lunged to the doorway. Bernie was headed toward the elevator, his suit jacket and briefcase in hand. Quickly, she grabbed her purse and her own jacket and scrambled after him. The elevator doors nearly slammed on her as she ducked into the car at the last possible moment.

Bernie, a tall, pasty, ungainly man, looked down at her, startled, his brown eyes widening in surprise…and something that looked suspiciously like dismay. "Cathy, you're back! But I thought…"

Could Hale be right about Bernie? The possibility that she was standing next to someone who had ransacked her apartment made her feel almost sick, but she plastered on a smile. "It's all right. We got married."

"But you and Bob were going on a big romantic honeymoon," he said. "Where was it?"

As if he didn't know! "The Cayman Islands."

"Oh, yes!" He slapped his forehead, making a big show of remembering. "I just got back from there not long ago."

"Bob told me." She watched him closely.

Bernie's gaze darted nervously around the elevator. He loosened his tie's iron grip around his thin turkey neck and turned back to her with a smile. "So...where is the old Bobster?"

Cathy forced a disappointed frown. "Wouldn't you know it? Bob caught a nasty cold the night before we were married! He won't be in for a week, but I decided there was no reason for both of us to be sitting idly around the house."

Bernie nodded his approval. "I'm the same way. If I'm in town, I have to work. I get restless. Can't stand sitting around watching 'Geraldo' all day."

A new bumper sticker slogan popped unbidden into Cathy's head. *I'D RATHER BE EMBEZZLING.*

A smile tugged at her lips. "You should call Bob, Bernie," she said, knowing he'd reach an answering machine. After she had ditched Hale and taken a reasonable nap, she'd gone by Bob's apartment and made up a new, perky outgoing message about their being newlyweds and instructing callers not to say anything after the beep unless it was very, very important. Bob's apartment had *not* been ransacked, which made her look with even more suspicion at Bernie. Bob might very well have informed his friend at some point that Cathy usually held on to their tickets—for plays, baseball games, you name it.

"Well, maybe I'll give old Bobster a buzz," he said,

jangling the change in his suit pocket nervously. "Maybe I'll zip by for a visit even. Tomorrow night, maybe. Yeah, tomorrow night."

She smiled. Something about the way he said tomorrow night made her certain that he absolutely wouldn't be paying a call on Bob. "That would cheer him up."

Bernie nodded. "Going home early?" It was only about four-fifteen.

"No, I thought I'd grab a snack," Cathy lied. "How about you? It's not like you to knock off before six."

"Oh, I have an errand to run. Shouldn't take long."

At the ground floor when the elevator belched out its passengers, Cathy hung back, allowing Bernie a small lead. Then she followed him, keeping about a half block's distance. She couldn't believe she was actually tailing someone, like Humphrey Bogart in those *films noir*. A private detective was never something she'd yearned to be, but she did feel a little buzz of excitement when, after ten minutes of walking, Bernie ducked inside a building. More interesting still, a few seconds later, a corpulent man with a beard stepped into the same doorway. The awning above the doorway read O'Leary's Pub.

Some errand! His running out to a bar certainly seemed suspicious, but Bernie had always possessed some vices that Bob, thankfully, was free of. In addition to drinking, Bernie would sometimes put a bet on a horse or a ball team, and he occasionally came out with jokes that Cathy deemed not entirely appropriate for mixed company. But most men were less circumspect than Bob in that respect. Bob, for instance, would never have remarked on the design or sheerness of her undergarments, as Hale had.

She frowned. *Why not?* Why wasn't Bob more interested in her...the way Hale was? She could see the twinkle of male appreciation in Hale's eyes when he looked at her.

Whenever she was alone with Bob, he always seemed more interested in PBS than sex. Why would he prefer Julia Child to herself?

When Bernie didn't come out of the bar immediately, Cathy grew bolder and edged toward the one window looking in on the dark room crowded with tables and chairs. Bernie wasn't at a table. She craned her neck, just able to see him at the bar—alongside the overweight man she'd seen follow him in. The two of them were talking. Was this a prearranged meeting?

It had to be. Bernie was very animated, yakking away while the large man listened. If only she could see what Bernie had brought in that briefcase, or hear their conversation! In the course of a quarter hour, Bernie tossed back two drinks, while his companion barely touched one. When the fat man reached into his back pocket to pay, Cathy scampered down the street and ducked into a doorway, out of sight, yet close enough to get a better gander at Bernie's friend. He left the bar ten seconds after Bernie, which solidified Cathy's hunch that something fishy was going on.

The overweight man was better dressed than Bernie. His gray suit was perfectly tailored to his huge frame, and his black shoes were polished to a high shine. The man obviously took pride in his appearance—a trait that softened Cathy's view of him. His dark beard was neatly trimmed, almost dapper. He reminded her of that late, great television actor, Sebastian Cabot, whose butler character on "Family Affair" had been a domestic guidepost of her childhood. *Her* family had desperately needed the tasteful, steadying hand of a butler like Mr. French.

Immediately, her mind started making up reasons why Bernie should have a secret meeting with the fat man. Maybe they were old friends, and the fact that they had entered and exited the bar ten seconds apart was just a coincidence. Or perhaps they were strangers who met by chance at this bar where Bernie had ducked in for an afternoon nip. It wasn't unthinkable.

Just unlikely. For one thing, Bernie had told her he was going on an errand. She had envisioned him picking up his dry cleaning. Yet just because he'd lied and met someone at a bar didn't necessarily connect the man to Bob's problem. Unless...

Was the fat man Dexter? Was *he* the man Bob was trying to tell her about?

Disappointed that she was no closer to solving Bob's problem, she trudged back to the office, lagging far behind Bernie. Master detective she was not; yet her jaunt had confirmed Bob's suspicion that Bernie was up to no good. She simply had to keep trying, or Bob might never be freed. If Bob weren't set free, they might never be married. And if she remained single much longer, and if Hale kept popping up at her door at odd hours, and if—God forbid!— they ever wound up naked together in a bed again...

She blushed with shame at the wicked thoughts parading across her imagination. As she pushed through the bank's revolving door she resolved to keep Hale and his devastating blue eyes and his sexy denim-clad butt firmly out of her mind.

She nodded to a janitor on the way to the elevator, but discovered to her dismay that his eyes reminded her of Hale's. *Was there no getting that man out of her head?* She tapped her navy blue pump impatiently as she waited for the elevator doors to slide open. Bob had blue eyes, too, yet the janitor hadn't reminded her of Bob. What was the matter with her? Why—

Narrowing her gaze, she pivoted and eyed the janitor again. He wore blue work pants, a matching cap, and a white shirt. Janitors at the FIB usually wore green coveralls.

His shirt had a patch with the name Jose sewn on it, yet this man looked about as Hispanic as Brad Pitt.

She walked up to him and crossed her arms, glaring in recognition. "Harriet!" Hale exclaimed. His face broke out into that now familiar, sexy grin. "I was wondering how long it would take you to see through my masterful disguise."

"How long have you been watching me?"

"Long enough to figure out that you've been following Bernie Morton."

"You've got a lot of nerve tailing me like a—" She did a mental double take. "How did you know that was Bernie?"

"Swithin described him for me," he said, adding in a more scolding tone, "I thought you agreed to leave the detecting to professionals."

She smirked. Professionals? "Is that what that outfit you have on makes you?"

Her criticism didn't faze him. Instead, he twirled good-naturedly for her benefit. "No holes in the pants, which are solid, neutral colored," he pointed out in a slightly lisping, mock designer voice. "The shirt is tasteful white, tucked in neatly, and contains no unsightly prints or slogans. I thought you of all people would appreciate my outfit, Cathy."

"I might, if you weren't wearing it for the express purpose of spying on me!"

He sighed and dropped the haute couture tone. "Okay, I was spying on you. And I found out that you're pretty good at this."

Her? She was amazed. "I am?"

He nodded. "They never spotted you outside that bar."

She felt a flush of pleasure and pride. Except, wasn't a

good detective supposed to know when someone was spying on *her?*

"Now I think it's time you told me what you know," he said.

She frowned at that request.

"There's no sense in us not sharing information. You think I don't want to figure this out the same way you do?"

"I suspect Bob's being under house arrest suits you fine."

"Why? Because I'm attracted to you?" he asked bluntly.

Her face felt as if it were on fire. "Well…yes."

"Then you suspect wrong. You're engaged to my brother. And as long as Bob is locked up like a fairy-tale princess, you're going to be his loyal knight errant."

First Joan, now Hale. Everyone seemed to take it for granted that once Bob was free the wedding would be cancelled! "Bob and I are going to be married."

He stared at her evenly. "Even if that were true," he said, clearly indicating he thought it wasn't, "you seem to be forgetting something even more important. It's my family's money that's being stolen. I owe it to my old man—however awful he's been to me in the past—to get to the bottom of this mess."

His father was more important to him than she was? Cathy didn't know why that statement should flabbergast her. Maybe because in her book Kevin Delaney ranked right up there with Attila the Hun in the charm department. And after all Hale's flirtation and banter and hints of jealousy of Bob, she had assumed she meant *something* to him.

She felt almost disappointed. Yet it wasn't as if she actually wanted Hale to fall in love with her. And he was offering to help her. She tried to think logically. Hale was a cop. He might know certain methods used in going about an investigation, whereas she barely knew where to begin.

He might be her best hope to get Bob back. "All right. I'll share what I know if you'll help me clear Bob. Where do we begin?"

He nodded toward the revolving door. "At Fifty-eighth Street and First Avenue," he said, ushering her toward the exit.

She gritted her teeth against the zip of electricity that passed through her at the merest touch of his hand on her arm. "What will we find there?"

His Paul Newmans twinkled irresistibly. "Pizza."

"SWEAR TO GOD," Cathy said, raising her right hand over a half-devoured slice of pizza, "that's all I know."

Hale frowned in thought as he chewed. "Bernie Morton acting nervous and having a drink with a dapper fat man isn't going to get us very far."

"I wonder if the fat man is the Mr. Dexter that Bob mentioned on the phone," Cathy said.

Hale's brows rose. "I wish he'd given a first name."

"Bob just said that if you were going to check out the computers at the bank, I should tell you about Dexter. And then he had to hang up."

Hale's face paled in recognition, and Cathy felt her pulse ratchet up a few notches. "Dexter isn't a person," he said suddenly. "He's a dog."

What? "I'm supposed to watch out for a dog? At the bank? That doesn't—"

Then, Cathy remembered. A year ago, when she had been thinking about adopting a puppy, Bob had told her about a Labrador he'd had in college and his twenties. Dexter! "But what could a dog have to do with the bank?"

Hale had it all figured out. "Don't you see? *Dexter* must be his password at work."

"I hate to disappoint you, Sherlock, but that's not it. I

jumped on his computer today, and his password is still what it's been for the past month. Eggcream.'' She took a swig of diet soda and finished, ''Besides, the way the bank system's set up, I don't need a password to search his directories and files. And Dexter wasn't among them.''

Hale wasn't discouraged by this news. In fact, for a moment he looked as if he'd just been struck with divine inspiration. ''In college, who did Bob share an apartment with?''

Cathy looked up. ''Bernie,'' she said, understanding. Dexter would have been Bernie's dog, too. ''That's it—maybe Dexter is a file in Bernie's computer!'' She glanced at her watch. It was nearly five forty-five. ''If we go back to the bank just before six, we won't have to sign in at the lobby. And most people in the offices will be going home.''

''But we'll have to sign out when we leave,'' Hale told her.

''Yes, but it's not unusual for me to work late. No one will think anything of it—and you can just give a fake name.''

He looked at her with playful affection. ''You're really getting the hang of this, aren't you?''

If there was a point in her life where time would freeze so that she would live that second for all eternity, Cathy might have chosen that one. She could have spent a blissful forever with her elbows propped up on a sticky Formica table, breathing in the doughy smell of the pizza shop, basking in Hale's admiring gaze. And she would be able to spend eternity guilt-free, too. Because Hale was just admiring her for her sleuthing skills. Nothing had really happened between them. Her feelings had nothing to do with how sexy Hale was. This was all about Bob.

As the last thought passed through her mind, however, it had a stale ring to it. Like when she was a kid and had to listen to her mother meditate all morning. After an hour or so of repetition, that mantra grew tiresome.

HALE SAT ON THE EDGE of the desk in Bernie Morton's dark office and leaned close enough to Cathy to smell the remnants of the perfume she'd dabbed on that afternoon. He watched her intent expression in the blue light of the computer screen and felt something hitch in his chest.

He tried to breathe steadily, to look at Cathy as if she were merely Bob's fiancée—a future relative. Yet he knew too much about her and Bob's lack of intimacy, and Bob's lack of enthusiasm for the wedding, to keep his feelings at bay. *Feelings* were the problem. He wasn't used to having this deep an attraction to any woman. Oh, he kept himself busy—guys around the precinct always had some woman or another to set him up with. But Hale had never found one woman he was interested in. Until he'd gone out and kidnapped one.

Cathy clucked her tongue and he forced himself to look at the computer screen. "Here we go," she said, having clicked to the prompt from which they could run a search of Bernie's directory and file names. She typed in the word *Dexter.*

"Aha!" Cathy cried triumphantly. "It's a subdirectory, Hale. We've got him!" She clicked her mouse on Dexter to call up the directory. But when the computer pulled up the directory, all the monitor revealed was a blank white screen.

"What's the matter?" Hale asked.

She sank back in her desk chair. "All the files in this directory have been moved."

He rubbed his jaw. "Maybe Bernie feared someone would start poking around. But at least we know that Bob was onto something. Maybe there's something around here that will give us an idea..."

Together, they began going through Bernie's things—his top desk drawer, his Rolodex, his day planner. Finally, Cathy pushed aside his computer keyboard and inspected the calendar desk blotter underneath. "Hale, look," she said, pointing to today's date. In the little square was written *4:30—M.H.* "That's the time we saw him at the bar with the fat man."

"The fat man must be M.H.," Hale said, flipping quickly now through the Rolodex until he reached the *H*s.

Cathy continued scanning the calendar but didn't have far to go. The very next night, Saturday, he had penned in, *Max's b-day—8:30 Windfall Towers.*

"There's a man named Maxwell Herbert here," Hale said, pulling out the card. "His address is in London." His brow puckered in thought. "Wait a sec... A few years ago, there was a Maxwell Herbert involved in a bribery case involving off-track betting officials. The cops never could make the evidence stick."

She pointed to the desk blotter. "Max is our man, apparently. And he's having a birthday tomorrow—at approximately the same time Bernie promised to drop in on his poor sick friend Bob for a visit. I thought he sounded like he was lying through his teeth, and now I know it. Do you think the Windfall Towers is an apartment building?"

Hale shook his head, and picked up the phone. "Not if my hunch is correct. You said Bernie gambles a little?"

She nodded.

"The Windfall Towers sounds suspiciously like a place in Atlantic City." When Information confirmed his hunch, he hung up the phone and grinned. "Ever crashed a birthday party?"

She shook her head. "And I'm not about to now, either. I can't show up there! What if Bernie saw me?"

Hale cocked his head. "How good are you with disguises?"

She sent his janitor's uniform a mirthful glance. "Not as good as you, I'm sure."

The urge to kiss the wry grin off her sweet lips was strong, but Hale managed to refrain. "I'm serious. No one will know who I am, but you will need to be transformed."

At that last word, the proverbial light bulb blinked on and Cathy smiled broadly. "I know just the place for that."

"Not your apartment," he said. "I don't want you staying alone tonight. In fact, why don't you spend the night in Brooklyn with me?"

Her lips parted, and her eyes looked levelly into his, as if she knew exactly where that idea would lead. Frankly, so did he.

"The place I have in mind is safe," she told him, but didn't say whether she meant safe from danger...or temptation.

In the next moments, they remained inches apart, swaying slightly in the blue light of the computer, looking into each other's eyes, each gauging how inappropriate a kiss would be. Every second he continued to look at Cathy's face, he felt that hitching sensation in his chest grow, until he felt that an iron band was squeezing his chest. Kiss her? He was almost afraid to move for fear his heart might burst.

She leaned away quickly. "We need to stop this."

"You want me not to be attracted to you?" Hale asked.

"Yes!" She tossed her head in confusion. "It's so senseless. I'm not the kind of woman you want."

"Oh, really? Because my body is definitely telling me otherwise."

"It is?" Her eyes widened and her gaze dropped to the

general direction of his zipper, then back up again. Two dots of color stained her cheeks, and this time she kept her gaze focussed on his eyes. "Well, if you do find me attractive…it's simply because you think I'm safe."

He practically howled. "Safe!" he cried. "Cathy, you're many things, but somebody who jumps into traffic and out on ledges is definitely not *safe.*"

She stiffened. "I only meant that because you're not a marrying man, and because we both know that I am absolutely about to walk down the aisle with your brother, you're looking at me as if I might be a harmless dalliance."

Dalliance. Yeah, sure. *That* explained the steel band squeezing his chest.

When he didn't say anything, but continued to stare at her, she twitched her hair nervously. "You see?" she said, her voice a squeak. "It's just… Well, my sister's a psychologist. I'm sure she could explain it better. You don't take me seriously."

"Yes, I do," he said, surprising himself. What was he doing? Next thing he knew he'd be dropping down on one knee—or ravishing her on Bernie Morton's desk.

She blinked. "I…we…" Words continued to fail her for a moment. "We need to call Bob!" she said, reaching for the phone. "Maybe he's heard of Max Herbert." She gave him the handset.

Bob, her security blanket. Hale punched in the numbers for his father's house in Connecticut and frowned. Of course, he wasn't being entirely truthful himself. Maybe he should tell Cathy that Bob wasn't quite as set on this marriage as she was. Maybe the woman should be given some warning… But it was Bob's job to call off his wedding, not Hale's.

"Hello!" a gravelly, too-familiar voice on the other end of the phone shouted.

"Dad," Hale said, disappointed. He'd been hoping Swithin would answer so he'd at least have a prayer of talking to Bob.

"Hale, you'd better have some pretty damn good news for me!" his father barked at him.

"Dad, I need to speak to Bob."

"So do I!" shouted Kevin Delaney.

Hale frowned. "Where is he?"

"How the hell should I know! He's run away!"

"Run away?"

Kevin Delaney huffed out a breath. "You heard me, Hale—I'm not going to sit here repeating myself like a damn lunatic!"

"Dad, calm down. When did Bob disappear?"

Cathy, listening, gasped.

"I don't know! The whole house is in an uproar. Bob's missing, Swithin's missing..."

"Swithin?" Hale asked, confused. It was hard for him even to imagine their butler off the estate. "Did they leave at the same time?"

"I have no idea! My men are still searching the area for them. No cars are missing."

"When was the last time anyone saw him?"

"How the hell should I know? Breakfast?"

"What's the matter?" Cathy was practically hopping up and down in suspense.

"Who's that?" his father barked into his ear.

"Cathy."

"Who?"

"Bob's fiancée," Hale reminded him.

"Her again!" Kevin exclaimed, growing even more agitated. "You keep an eye on that one. I wouldn't be surprised if she helped Bob escape!"

"Dad, I don't think so."

"He never ran off with my butler before."

Hale almost laughed. "I wouldn't worry about Bob picking up bad habits right now, Dad. Just track him down—and keep me posted." He hung up the phone. "Bob is missing," he told Cathy.

She stared at him as if trying to make sense of the startling news, then broke into a smile. "He escaped!"

"Maybe." Hale remembered the last time he'd seen Bob, who had been in no hurry to leave the mansion. And what about Swithin?

She looked anxious. "What do you think happened to him?"

"I imagine the only way we'll find out for sure is by tracking down Max Herbert in Atlantic City tomorrow."

Cathy sucked in her breath as a terrible thought occurred to her. "Oh, Hale—you don't think Bob really is in cahoots with the bad guys, do you?"

He couldn't believe that after all this time she was entertaining the possibility that Bob's character might be less than sterling—especially when he had drawn the opposite conclusion. "No, I don't," he said. "But I'm beginning to think my father's faith in his butler might have been misplaced."

8

"I LIKE YOU MUCH BETTER as a blonde!" Joan exclaimed. "Honestly, Cath, I could do wonders with some permanent dye!"

"No thanks," Cathy said, tossing her head from side to side to get the feel of her newly installed hair. It was longer than she was used to—and definitely more flamboyant. She had to admit, she looked different, which was good. If she was going to Atlantic City, where she might come face to face with Bernie Morton, she needed to look unrecognizable. But did she have to look like Farrah Fawcett with her finger in a light plug?

"Well…it's snug," she said in the wig's defense.

Joan nodded. "That's because you've got more pins in you than a voodoo doll. But we've simply *got* to do something about that makeup!"

"I barely wear any."

Her sister rolled her eyes disapprovingly. "That's what I mean. We've got to fluff you up."

Cathy couldn't imagine being much more fluffy, unless she were a poodle at the Westminster dog show. But fifteen minutes later, with the help of some hot pink lipstick and sky blue eyeshadow, her transformation was complete…or so she thought.

"Now for the final touch!" Joan practically skipped to her closet, from which she extracted a wrap dress in a shade of green that Cathy hadn't seen since 1978. "These are all the rage now—and *this* is a vintage Halston!"

Cathy sucked in her breath. "My God, it's awful."

Joan blinked. "I thought you'd like it… I've got another one done in a violet print on a beige background, if you'd rather—"

Knowing the lesser of two evils when she saw it, Cathy snatched the green dress from her sister's grasp and put it on fast. Some things were best done quickly, like diving into icy water. It was easier to handle the shock that way.

But when she looked into the mirror, she didn't scream in horror, or burst into hysterical laughter as she'd feared she would. Just the idea of wearing old clothes, something that had been forced on her when she was young, usually gave her the willies. To be wearing vintage seventies would normally have sent her into nervous collapse. But as she inspected herself now, she was able to put the matter into perspective and even enjoy looking so different from her usual beige and navy self.

"What about shoes?"

Joan was delighted. "I've got a pair that match!"

Cathy tilted her head critically, inadvertently setting off an avalanche of blond curls. "You don't think I'll stick out?"

"Believe me," Joan assured her, "no one in Atlantic City will look twice at you…except, of course, the men. I never thought I'd be saying this, Cathy, but you're a knock-out."

That observation did almost reduce her to hysterical laughter. "I don't *want* men to be looking at me too closely," she said. "Especially this guy from the bank. If he recognizes me, I'm done for."

Joan chuckled. "Don't worry about that. No one would

confuse you for Cathy Seymour. If I were you, I'd just have fun exploring this other side of yourself."

Cathy shivered. She hated it when Joan spoke about people having all sorts of different sides—as if everyone had a multiple personality disorder just waiting to burst forth. And yet, as she sashayed around her sister's apartment in her wig and slinky dress, she couldn't help wondering if there weren't some truth to the theory. In the past two days, she'd done all sorts of things she never imagined herself capable of. She felt different, more daring. And what was most surprising, for the first time in her life, she didn't feel so afraid of that free spirit lurking inside her. Maybe this time, if it decided to make an appearance, she could use it to her advantage.

"I think I might enjoy playing vamp for a day," she said, taking off the dress and changing into a nightshirt she'd brought from her apartment.

Joan, who had met Hale when he delivered Cathy to her door, clucked her tongue knowingly. "I can see why vamping around Hale would appeal to you..."

For a moment Cathy hesitated about whether to confide in her sister, but couldn't resist. Her behavior with Hale preyed on her mind. And her conscience. She cleared her throat. "There's, um, something I didn't mention the other night. About Hale and me."

Joan practically leapt on her. "What? You have to tell me!"

Cathy felt silly for blushing. "He kissed me..."

Joan looked breathless. "And?"

"And tonight, he said that he was still very attracted to me, physically."

Joan nearly jumped for joy, and actually tossed a pillow in the air. "Hallelujah!"

At her sister's reaction, Cathy recoiled. Even though the

kiss had set off a similar jubilation in her own heart, it had lasted only briefly. "Joan, this is serious—it's horrible!"

"You should be celebrating. Hale's a great guy."

"You don't even know him," Cathy argued, although of course she agreed. "And what about Bob? He thinks we're going to be married—I mean, we *are* going to be married."

Her sister raised a skeptical brow. "Oh, really."

"Bob is counting on me."

"How do you know?" Joan asked.

Cathy bridled uncomfortably. "Because Bob is steady and solid and—"

"Madly, passionately in love with you?"

Cathy blinked. "Well, not exactly…" Was he? For that matter, was Hale? Her mind reeled in confusion. "Anyway, he's *missing*. He's not here to defend himself. What should I do?"

Her sister took a breath. "You really want my opinion?"

Unbelievable as it seemed, she did. Cathy nodded.

"All shrinking aside, honey, I say you and Hale should go for it!"

Cathy sank onto the sofa bed and sighed. *Go for it* was precisely what her hormones were telling her to do. It had been all she could manage not to *go for it* right there on top of Bernie Morton's desk. "But there's Bob to consider, not to mention that father of theirs! I think there's insanity in the family."

"Cathy, this is fate. Go for it."

"Would you stop saying that? Hale is Bob's brother."

Joan shrugged. "Believe me, my patients have told me stranger tales. *Much* stranger."

"That's not much consolation."

Joan sat down next to her. "What's really bothering you?"

"It's just…none of this is remotely normal," Cathy said.

"What would have happened if I *hadn't* been kidnapped? Would Bob and I be married and living happily ever after?"

"Maybe," Joan admitted. "Or maybe you would have been living miserably ever after."

Cathy thought of another, equally chilling scenario. "Or maybe I would have met Hale two or three years down the line..."

Joan nodded. "And would it have been any different? Could you really imagine seeing Hale and not falling in love with him?"

Love?

Cathy jumped, for the first time understanding that expression about flipping one's wig. "Who said anything about love?" She hopped off the bed and marched to the bathroom to scrub off her makeup. *Love!* That was something a person didn't just feel after two days of knowing someone. Besides which, she doubted Hale Delaney had ever felt love for any woman. "The man can't even remember the names of his old girlfriends."

Joan followed her as far as the bathroom door, which she leaned against while watching Cathy in the bathroom mirror. "I *saw* the way he looked at you."

"How?" As if she had to ask! She knew the look Joan was talking about. Those blue bedroom eyes had a way of gazing at her that made her shiver right down to the tips of her toes. She'd never wanted a man so much. She'd never had a man want *her* so much. She was afraid there was no way she could *not* "go for it."

"You really want to know?" Joan asked.

Did she? Tomorrow she and Hale would be in Atlantic City, alone together, maybe for the last time. The temptation to "go for it" might be unbearable. She didn't need to spend the night thinking about Hale, dwelling on how he looked at her, and getting herself more steamed up than necessary.

Yet, always a glutton for punishment, Cathy slapped cold cream on her face and nodded for her sister to continue.

"Like he was dehydrated and you were a water cooler."

Joan's description nearly brought tears to her eyes—as if those words somehow sealed her fate. For the fact of the matter was, Bob had *never* looked at her as if she were a water cooler.

Oh, Bob! she thought mournfully. *Would he ever forgive her?*

"HALE..." CATHY MUTTERED through pink lips as they walked into the glaring opulence of the lobby of the Windfall Towers Hotel. "People are staring."

Hale laughed. "*Men* are staring—at you, sweetheart." And he felt like punching the lights out of every one of them.

But what man in his right mind wouldn't look at her? She was flashy and sexy in her blond wig and a dress that hugged her curves—curves that, given the boxy suits he'd seen her in before, had only been a matter of speculation. Now there was no guessing about it. It was almost impossible for him to take his eyes off her. They had spent the entire trip from Manhattan in the confines of his Jeep, silent and preoccupied by the fact that Bob had not been found overnight. Hale had to force himself to keep his gaze on the road and off the beguiling hint of cleavage her wrap dress allowed him.

For his part, he was dressed more conservatively in black slacks, loafers, and a white T-shirt underneath a plaid jacket. Around his neck he wore two gold chains. Hale figured he and Cathy were a matching pair, but Cathy was the real draw. A man would have to be blind not to stare at her. Hale just wished he had a trenchcoat that he could throw over her.

He looked ahead to the front desk. "This is it. Act natural."

In answer to Hale's directive, Cathy pushed her oversized round sunglasses up to the crown of her windblown wig and laughed. "How am I supposed to act natural in a pair of funky platform shoes high enough for Greg Louganis to swan dive off?"

Hale took her arm in his and smiled. Frankly, he wouldn't have minded if the day lasted forever. Chances were, this trail would lead him to the embezzlers, and they would find Bob, and then…who knew what would happen? If Cathy had her way, their short-lived relationship would be history.

Just the thought of losing her caused his heart to squeeze painfully. He'd only kissed her once, and yet he craved her like a drug. Her wry humor, her strange way of looking at things, even her prickliness—he couldn't imagine not having her in his life now. He vowed that before the day was over, they would have a talk about them…and about Bob. He wasn't going to try to seduce her. Kissing her only seemed to make her nervous. They didn't have much time, and he wanted to deal with her on her own terms, with logic. They could discuss the pros and cons of him versus his brother. They could discuss the long term.

He glanced over at her and felt a lump in his throat. The trouble was, with her looking like that, he didn't exactly feel like talking. He felt like taking her in his arms and *showing* her why she shouldn't marry Bob.

He stopped at the front desk, forcing his attention away from Cathy and onto the matter at hand. "Where is Max Herbert's party tonight?"

The clerk, a young pimply fellow who, in Hale's opinion,

seemed overly interested in Cathy's bust, forced his gaze down to the black planner in front of him. "In the ballroom. Eight-thirty."

The pipsqueak then focused his attention on Cathy's legs—practically draped himself over the marble front desk to ogle them, in fact. Hale cleared his throat. "We'd like a room, please."

The desk clerk, red-faced, snapped back to attention. "A room? We're all booked."

"We'll take anything you have, naturally," Hale said, knowing that there was a difference between booked and filled.

"As long as it's got a king-size bed," Cathy blurted out.

Hale turned to her, stunned. Where had she come up with that? "I don't think it matters, does it?"

Cathy, to his surprise, was throwing her heart and soul into her bimbo role. She laughed suggestively. "Course it does, darlin'. Don't you always say you like it best when we have plenty of room?" She winked a false eyelash at him and turned back to the desk clerk. "C'mon, hon, a place like this is bound to have something. We've got four hours till the party starts—we got to have something to do!"

"Uh..." The clerk's jaw hung open. "I don't know..."

"Or how about one of those neat rooms with a heart-shaped bed or something like that?" Cathy went on.

The pimply kid's red face was now almost purple. "A theme room?"

"That's it, a theme room!" Cathy cried happily. "Think you can manage one of those?"

"We *do* have the Tahitian suite available," he said to Hale, who was feeling rather red-faced himself. He hadn't expected Cathy to ham it up so authentically.

"Tahiti!" Cathy let out a little shriek and hopped up and

down, like a contestant who'd just won the grand prize on "Wheel of Fortune."

Hale shook his head in amazement. "That will be fine," he told the clerk. He signed them in as Harold and Harriet Hughes from Queens. Cathy inspected the register and her smile widened.

"I didn't know you were such a good actress," Hale said as they rode up alone in the elevator.

One brow darted up on her forehead. "What do you mean?"

"Your routine at the front desk. You know—about the room."

She blinked at him, managing to appear the perfect image of innocence and suggestiveness all at once. "Well... what *were* we going to do for four whole hours?"

The doors swished open and she sashayed through them, swinging her hips in a way that made Hale's mouth go bone dry. He stumbled after her, not sure quite what to expect next. The only thing he was dead certain of now was that Cathy wasn't feeling quite herself today.

The Tahitian suite proved more than deserving of its name. Not only was the room littered with potted palms, all the furniture had what appeared to be a coconut shell finish. The floor was done in thick-piled green carpet, and the walls, incongruously, were covered in gold wallpaper with a white flocked design. The canopied bed was draped in netting and covered with a wild jungle-print bedspread.

Hale and Cathy stood in the doorway, their eyes popping in amazement. Finally, Hale hazarded a step inside. "C'mon, Harriet, I'm sure the natives are friendly."

She followed him, slowly, gaping at the imitation Gauguin paintings on the walls, of exotic, bare-breasted women. "Good heavens!" she exclaimed, turning in a circle. "It's like something out of a horror movie..."

Hale nodded. "All that's missing are the nuclear mosquitoes."

"I guess that's what the net canopy around the bed's supposed to protect us from."

She kicked off her platform shoes and headed for that king-size bed…the last place Hale wanted to envision her. He was already keyed up enough from bouncing around in a Jeep with her all day, so close and yet unable to touch her, without having to watch her loll on the bed. He turned back to the door, trying to think of anything to get them out of the room—and get his mind off sex. They couldn't really start their investigation until later, when Max Herbert and his party would be preoccupied with their birthday soiree.

"How about a little gambling?" he suggested. "We could lose all our money before dinner."

"No thank you! I've never been one for that kind of thing."

No, of course not. She hated uncertainty. But the only certainty Hale knew was that if they stayed in this room, he would try to seduce his brother's fiancée.

"How about a stroll on the boardwalk, then?" His voice cracked with desperation. He heard the soft sound of her shapely bottom making contact with the mattress. If he didn't get out of there soon, he might start clawing the flocked wallpaper.

"No thanks." She looked at him, her eyes dark with something he could have sworn was desire, and smiled. "Hale, why don't you relax?" She turned to the bedstand and started fiddling with the light dimmer.

"I am relaxed," he said stiffly. But as the room became washed in a dull, sensual glow, he felt as wound up as a yo-yo and turned to inspect the interior of the closet. *What about talking?* he thought as he thumbed through the un-removable coat hangers. *What about thinking long-term?*

"You don't seem relaxed," she purred from the bed. "Why don't you—"

In a split second, her seductive question turned into a piercing shriek, sending Hale spinning on his heel. A whir-ring noise filled the air, and Cathy had gone into spasms on the bed—which undulated out of control beneath her!

"Hale, make it stop!" she cried, flailing an arm toward the nightstand. Her dress was hiked up almost to her hips as she struggled to get upright on the soft, vibrating mat-tress, and her bare feet kicked the air helplessly. "It's alive!"

And it looked as if it just might swallow her. Hale's protective adrenaline kicked into high gear. He saw a con-trol on the headboard and dived aboard the ornery bed, not quite prepared himself to maneuver across the electrically storm-tossed mattress. On all fours, he scrambled across the bedspread, crawled over Cathy, and finally flicked the switch to Off. The maverick mattress stilled.

"Oh my goodness!" Cathy exclaimed as Hale half col-lapsed on top of her. "What was *that* all about?"

Hale let out a laugh. "Magic fingers."

"More like a magic mauling!" Cathy exclaimed.

Hale took a breath. Cathy was still sprawled with her dress hiked up her thighs and, incidentally, almost spilling open at her cleavage. He took another deep, bracing intake of air that did nothing to quell the arousal the sight of her soft swelling breast caused.

He couldn't believe they were lying in bed to-gether...and that Cathy didn't seem to mind one bit. She swallowed, drawing Hale's attention to the delicate, swan-like curve of her neck. He itched to bend down and place a light kiss at the hollow at her collarbone. Instead, he shifted his weight against her, leaving her no doubt concerning the state of his desire.

Her eyes widened with surprise. She struggled to prop herself up on her elbows. "Well, let's see," she said in a poor attempt at matter-of-factness. "What were you saying about going to the boardwalk?"

Cannon fire wouldn't blast him off this bed now. "You weren't interested," Hale reminded her.

"Oh, right. I was going to take a..." She looked away from him. "Nap. Or..." As she began to absorb his proximity, her body became more rigid. "What were you saying about gambling?"

"You don't gamble," he informed her. "You don't like taking any kind of chances, remember?"

"No, of course not..." But the gaze she sent him told him that she knew lying in this bed was dicier than any gaming table could be.

When he looked into her eyes, so soft and vulnerable, he himself felt as lost to impulse as a compulsive gambler would be in front of a slot machine. He wanted to tell her all that he felt for her, in spite of how much he knew he shouldn't. He wanted to tell her that she shouldn't marry his brother when she was in love with himself, but he feared the instant he mentioned Bob's name, this fragile moment would be over.

Somehow he had to try to communicate that his need for her went beyond desire—even if he doubted that she would believe it. "Cathy, there's something I've wanted to do all day, but I—"

"Me, too," she said.

He continued to look into her brown eyes. "Really?" Maybe she also thought it was time to talk things over. "What?"

''This.'' With a hand on each of his lapels, she pulled him down flush against her, and pressed her lips to his.

THE MOMENT THEIR LIPS touched, Cathy felt her entire body relax. All day she had been gearing herself up to seduce Hale, and now she knew she wasn't wrong to follow her sister's advice. This felt right. Hale felt right.

It hadn't been as difficult as she'd feared it would be, either. As was usual in their short relationship, calamity—this time in the form of magic fingers—had brought them together, and from there taking the initiative had seemed easy, almost inevitable. Now that they were a jumble of arms and legs and clothes more off than on, she couldn't envision having a moment of regret.

His tongue entwined with hers and she released a soft moan of pleasure. She felt so achy with need she was half tempted to beg him to make wild, frenzied love to her immediately. But her more reasonable half wanted to selfishly hoard every second, to attempt to make each moment last a millennium.

Cathy splayed her hands against his chest. She wanted to see his eyes, to ensure that the same fire was consuming them both. ''I wish we were spending the night here, Hale,'' she whispered. ''I wish we had four months instead of four hours.''

It was obvious she could have knocked him over with a toucan feather, but the darkness in his eyes let her know her words pleased him. ''So do I.''

She stared boldly into his eyes. ''I think I want to make love with you.''

''I know so,'' he said, bending down to satisfy the urge to nibble at her neck. The little nips sent a shiver through her.

She felt a moment of shyness as his hand reached to open

the top of her dress. "I've never made love in the after-noon," she told him, her lips inches from his.

His blue eyes narrowed. "Serious?"

It did seem a serious omission in her life experience now that she was poised on the edge of something she sensed would be wonderful beyond belief. She grinned and wriggled against him sensually. "I'm not opposed to the idea, however."

He smiled back, and moved to untie her dress, but she stopped him by untucking the T-shirt from his pants. She then pulled his chains over his head, and, twirling them around her finger, tossed them across the room. After that, she pulled up his shirt, discarded it, and splayed her hands across his naked chest.

His breathing felt ragged. How could someone like Hale, who seemed so self-assured and sexy, suddenly seem so vulnerable to her? She felt she had a newly discovered power, and she wanted to wield it in the most deliberate way, before she was lost forever in the fire she felt building inside her. She reached down, unzipped and pushed down his pants and began to stroke him gently. His eyes closed and the muscles of his jaw tightened. He was rigid with velvety heat beneath her fluttery caresses, and his barely checked desire only made her own build more.

"Cathy." His voice was raspy, deep.

He pulled her close for another kiss, and she felt in that moment that she wouldn't mind never coming up for air again. She moved against him needfully, the friction of her breasts against his bare chest nearly driving her to distraction.

He undid her top and pushed it down, revealing a sheath-thin black bra that she had purposefully picked that morning. From the appreciative glint in his eye, she saw that she had not chosen wrong. He sucked in his breath, then reached down to unhook the front closure. It fell away like wispy clouds before a wind, revealing her to him. He bent and kissed one taut peak, teasing it with his tongue.

Cathy put her hands on his shoulders, and together they fell back against the pillows, a tangle of arms and legs, exploring each other with a hunger Cathy had never experienced before. She had known that Hale was virile and sexy as hell, and suspected that he was probably an expert in the art of pleasing a woman in bed, but she hadn't anticipated how he would make *her* feel. She suddenly felt expert, too—or at least she knew precisely what she wanted. And she wasn't at all hesitant to make her hungry curiosity known.

Neither was he. Just when she thought she might be lost forever to the momentum of their passion, he pulled back and smiled at her. ''I have to do one thing,'' he said, pulling her up to a sitting position.

She didn't know what to expect—and, more surprisingly, felt no desire to object to whatever it was he was about to propose. When his hands reached for her hair and started unpinning the wig from her head, she smiled. She'd completely forgotten about it.

He tossed aside the blond tresses and ran his fingers through her short brown hair as if it were spun from pure silk. ''Your hair is beautiful,'' he whispered. ''*You're* beautiful. I had to see all of you.''

Then, as she had tossed aside his own clothes and chains, he set about discarding her clothes. He pushed her dress, panties and hose down her long legs and tossed them away from the bed, then did the same with his remaining garments. When he looked back at her and she saw the loving, almost possessive glint in his eye as she lay naked before him, she felt a new, stronger arousal.

He parted her thighs with a gentle pressure, revealing the

most intimate part of her. She let out another soft moan and yielded to his tender ministrations—until she was ready for more. She reached up and pulled him toward her until he was positioned just at the brink of entering her.

Hale pulled back, hesitating. "Cathy, I—"

But Cathy lifted a finger to his lips and stopped him from saying another word. For once in her life, she *wanted* to be rash. She didn't want to talk, or plan, or give herself a final chance to be sensible. Neither did she want to wake up in the morning, as she had that one time in Mexico, and realize that she'd made a mistake—she wanted to make the mistake with her eyes already open, and enjoy herself.

With a gentle lift of her hips, she brought him inside her. It was only a subtle movement, but it felt like an explosion, after which there was no turning back, no salvaging any particle of rational thought. The soft friction was past bearing, and they moved together instantly and in a growing frenzy until Tahiti was blotted out completely and all Cathy saw were stars and comets and Hale's handsome face clenched taut in ecstasy.

9

CATHY NUZZLED AGAINST Hale's chest and swayed lazily as a piano lounge singer crooned "The Man I Love" in the corner of the dimly lit hotel bar. The place smelled of stale beer, the amp system crackled, and the singer wasn't very good, but Cathy didn't care. To her, a more beautiful song had never been written. Peggy Lee couldn't have sung it better. And she'd never been in as lovely a place as the Windfall Towers Hotel in Atlantic City, New Jersey.

"It's eight thirty," Hale whispered in her ear.

"Mmmm." They'd been draped over each other for nearly an hour, barely moving.

"We need to get to work."

Cathy stared at him through passion-glazed eyes. Her legs still felt wobbly beneath her from their afternoon of lovemaking, as if expressing all the love she felt for Hale had drained every drop of energy from her bones. "One more song?"

"That's what you said five songs ago," he reminded her.

And it was the same thing she would say five songs into the future. She never wanted to let him go. Taking a shaky breath, she looked into those dazzling blue eyes. "Okay," she said. "I'll take off my Ginger Rogers hat now. Reluctantly."

He nodded. "Put on your Watson hat."

"Aye, aye, Sherlock."

Hale laughed. "Watson with a parrot on his shoulder."

They stumbled back out into the bright lights of the lobby and headed once again for the front desk. The leering clerk of that afternoon had vanished, replaced by a rather bored-looking man in his twenties, who appeared more interested in getting back to the well-thumbed Stephen King tome at his elbow than any question a guest might ask.

Hale nodded at the young man.

"Yeah?" the guy asked, then sputtered apologetically, "I mean, yes, sir? May I help you?"

"We want to send a drink up to Max Herbert's room. Can you arrange that for us?"

The young man nodded toward a bank of three phones along the connecting wall. "There are our courtesy phones, sir. You can order room service from any one of them."

"And what is Mr. Herbert's room number?"

The desk clerk lackadaisically punched the name into his computer. "Suite Ten-A."

Hale grinned. "Thanks."

Hale and Cathy went over to the phones the guy had pointed them to. Hale picked up the receiver and spoke in an authoritative voice. "I'd like a bottle of your best champagne sent to Suite Ten-A, please."

So far, so good. When he'd hung up the phone, they waited anxiously for the elevator to take them to the tenth floor. As they were standing, another man joined them. A very familiar man.

Cathy froze. This was the moment she'd been dreading. Bernie Morton, dressed neatly in a suit and tie but smelling strongly of bourbon, squinted at Cathy for a moment, obviously trying to place her. She turned and draped herself around Hale, hoping her anxiety didn't show in her face. Hoping her appearance was disguised enough. Hale bent down and planted a kiss full on her lips, and she clung to

him for a moment, nearly losing her fears in the warmth
and strength of his arms. Nearly.

The elevator doors slid open, and the three of them got
on. Hale punched the button for ten, then turned politely to
Bernie, who stood stooped in a corner. "What floor?"

Bernie smiled, looking from Cathy to Hale. "Six."

During the silent trip to the sixth floor, Cathy's heart was
in her throat. She prayed her heavy makeup made her look
enough unlike herself to repel any suspicions. She hoped
her wig was on straight. She wished she had some chewing
gum to smack on or a cigarette—anything to release some
nervous energy! She was certain Bernie was peeping at her
out of the corner of his eye.

After the elevator finally deposited Bernie on six, she
collapsed against Hale. "Do you think he recognized me?"

Hale shook his head. "I hope not."

Hope! "If he did, he'll know something's up. Why
would I be traipsing around in Atlantic City in a wig just
days after my wedding, without Bob?" She started hyper-
ventilating. "I knew this was a bad idea! What were we
thinking? We should go back to New York! Let's call the
police!"

Hale shook his head as they disembarked on ten. "Will
you calm down? Everything will be just fine."

"Fine?" Cathy whispered, her voice a low hiss. Her ankles wobbled atop her platform shoes. "Oh, sure—Bob is
missing, I'm running around looking like a floozy, and Bernie Morton is four floors down, probably wondering why
his best friend's wife is disguised, hanging on a stranger's
arm, and headed for Max Herbert's suite."

"There are other rooms on the tenth floor," Hale whispered as they stopped in front of Suite Ten-A.

She looked at him skeptically. "He knows—I know he
knows. He was staring at me funny."

Hale laughed. "Because you look like a floozy."

She sent him a withering glare.

"Would you calm down?" he said, gently rubbing the small of her back in a way that had the exact opposite effect. If only she could make her teeth stop chattering! "We can't turn back now. Soon we might have the whole thing figured out."

"Or we might be dead."

The elevators opened down the hall and both of them straightened. Cathy looked up at Hale, trying to remember the key routine they'd practiced to get them into Max Herbert's room.

"You don't have it?" she asked suddenly.

Hale blinked. Then, remembering the act, he started patting his jacket and fishing into his pockets just as the room service guy swung around the corner with a cart bearing a bottle of champagne on ice. "I must have left it."

She rolled her eyes. "Oh, Max, you bungler! Can't you remember anything?"

He waggled a finger in her face. "Don't start with me, Harriet—"

"This is the *third* time you've locked us out of our room!"

The room service waiter stopped and stood by awkwardly.

"All we have to do is call down and get another key."

"*Call* from where?" Cathy practically shrieked. "We're locked out! You can bet I'm not the one who'll be traipsing down to the lobby. You can just go yourself!"

The waiter finally piped up, "I have a key, Mr. Herbert."

Hale turned to the man and smiled, then glared back at Cathy-Harriet. "The waiter has a key," he informed her unnecessarily. "Why do you have to fly off the handle all the time?"

"*I* fly off the handle?" Cathy yelled. "Ha! That's a laugh! You're the one who embarrassed us at dinner last night."

The dinner argument continued while the waiter ushered them into their room, popped open the champagne, received his twenty-dollar tip from Hale, and slunk back out into the hallway.

When he was gone, Cathy sank onto a bed with a fleur-de-lis coverlet. "I can't believe we're here..." Then she gaped around the room in wonder. This room was as elaborately done as the Tahitian suite, only the theme was pulled from the other half of the world. "...in Paris."

"*Mais oui,*" Hale answered in a deadpan voice. "And we're not finished yet." He began throwing open closets and drawers.

She got up and moved past a mural of the Champs-Elysées into the next room—a sitting room that was supposed to resemble a fashionable salon. The French provincial furniture was way overdone, but on the cream-and-gold table by the window, she saw exactly what she was looking for. A laptop case!

She ran over to it, unzipped the protective cover and pulled the computer out. After it was booted up, she said a quick prayer and logged on to the system. After scrolling down three pages, her gaze alit on the magic word. *Dexter*.

"Hale!"

He came running in and knelt beside her as she went to the file. At the click of a button, the screen filled with listings of files. Hale moused to the name *Delaney* and clicked. A page of graphs came up, followed by several more pages of dates of bank transactions.

"This is it," Hale said. "A record of withdrawals from the First International Bank. Dad's accountant was right. He's been skimming interest out of the Delaney trust and depositing it in a bank account overseas. In the Cayman Islands, no doubt.''

Cathy frowned as she quickly slipped in a disk and copied the file. "But *who?*" she asked. "Who's been doing it? Bernie Morton? Max Herbert? Bob?"

Hale frowned. "I can't imagine that it would take three men to embezzle from one account."

A terrible idea occurred to Cathy. She had been so focussed on the Delaneys' problem, she hadn't really considered the possibility of a broader spectrum of theft inside the First International Bank. "Oh, Hale," she breathed, hardly able to conceive of what they might have stumbled upon. "All those other names..."

They went back into the other files and found similar records of transactions—thousands of dollars withdrawn over a period of six months from accounts worth millions. The increments were small enough to escape notice by the account holders for a period of months. Enough to get the money—and possibly the thief—safely overseas.

"There's enough salami slicing in that place to open a delicatessen," Hale noted wryly as Cathy copied all she could onto one disk.

"Oh, Bob..." she whispered sadly. Could he really be a part of this? Why else would he have disappeared without a trace?

She looked up at Hale and handed him the computer disk.

"Look, Cathy, Bob told me he was innocent, and I believe him."

"But what about that change in our honeymoon plans to the Cayman Islands?" she asked. "He's probably there right now, without me! He probably knew all along that he was going to change destinations—and all that time he had me convinced he wanted to go to Amish country!"

Hale looked at her searchingly. "Maybe this isn't the time, but there was something else I didn't tell you about what Bob said to me. I should have told you this afternoon. Or even earlier..."

She frowned at the serious look in his eye, and felt a lump form in her stomach. He was about to tell her bad news, she knew that much. "You don't have to hide anything from me, Hale."

"When I talked to Bob about you, and the wedding, he said—"

"Okay you two!"

Both Hale and Cathy, absorbed in the drama of their conversation, jumped at the sound of the rough, accented voice. When they turned, startled, a man was standing alone in the doorway. Cathy felt her face go slack with amazement. *"Bob!?"*

His blue eyes were owl wide beneath his glasses. He wore a blue suit, one of the same ones he'd worn to work every day of his life, yet he appeared uncomfortable, not like himself at all. His mouth dropped open as he digested Cathy's getup. *"Cathy?"*

Her heart sank. What was he doing here? Was he a part of an embezzling racket? Is that what Hale had been on the verge of divulging to her?

Before she could speak, Bob lost his balance, as if pushed, and stumbled toward her awkwardly. Cathy caught him by the arms and propped him back up, suddenly noticing the sweat on his brow—and the three men who had followed him into the small room.

First there was Swithin, looking oilier than ever in a dark gray suit and shiny shoes that seemed to match his slicked-back hair. It was the first time she'd ever seen him out of his bathrobe. Behind him was Bernie—looking sheepish.

And finally in waddled Max Herbert himself, perfectly manicured and wielding a very large gun.

Cathy's heart raced uncontrollably, and she glanced at Hale. He gave her a guarded look, yet one so full of love and reassurance that she turned back to the man with the gun, her chin lifted, hoping that her fear didn't show in her face.

Hale directed anger toward his old family retainer. "Swithin, you traitor! All that malarkey you handed me about butlers and their code, and never needing thanks."

Swithin's thin lips turned up in a slight sneer. "I simply forgot to add that every once in a while we require a bit of a payoff."

"You're an ingrate."

Even in the face of insults, Swithin's emotions appeared as implacable as his pomaded hair. "I am what you say, Mr. Hale, but then what does that make you? You turned on your father years ago."

Cathy could feel Hale's body stiffen. "I didn't steal from him," he said. "I didn't betray his trust."

"The poor man was bereft when you left home," Swithin said. "I merely took his money, which ordinarily he wouldn't even have noticed. In fact, no one noticed Bernie's original paltry theft except me. Not even your father's accountant."

Bernie slumped uncomfortably, his face white. "I didn't intend to take much, I really didn't."

Swithin grinned. "But when I approached you and advised you to be more bold, you didn't hesitate, did you?" Bernie looked miserable, and the butler shook his head. "Bernie here wants you to think he's suffered the tortures of the damned, when really he's been laughing all the way to the bank since I introduced him to Uncle Max."

"Your uncle!" Hale exclaimed.

Swithin grinned. "It never occurred to you that a mere *servant* might have relatives in high places?"

"High in the underworld, maybe," Hale replied stiffly.

"That's good enough for me." He turned to his infamous relative. "Uncle Max, meet another son of my former employer, Mr. Hale Delaney. Oh, and the woman is…" He sniffed distastefully. "Mr. Bob's fiancée."

Max Herbert grinned, revealing a straight row of foxy white teeth, and said in a clipped English accent, "Smashing girl, but not very bright, is she? If her disguise couldn't even make it past Bernie…"

In spite of her fear, Cathy hadn't lived twenty-eight years to be dismissed as a *girl*, smashing or otherwise, by some gun-wielding thug. As for *her* intelligence… "Do you think you aren't going to be caught, Mr. Herbert? I've got a disk that can prove your guilt!"

He laughed. "How convenient. But I'm afraid you're quite mistaken on one point. *You're* the one who's caught."

Cathy's thoughts raced in growing panic, and as she glanced from the gun in Max's hand, back to Bob, then to a stone-faced Hale and then back to the gun, they whirled with growing ferocity around one idea: *escape.*

Caught? Not yet, she wasn't! She spun around, grabbed her handbag off the computer table, and ran as fast as her green platform shoes would carry her.

"Catch her!" Max yelled from behind her.

There was only one room in the suite to run to, which was another bedroom. She prayed there was another door there—and there was! The Eiffel Tower was decoratively painted on it. She ran toward the Parisian landmark as if her life depended on it—which it just might. She could outrace Bernie, she was sure. But when she glanced back, it wasn't her old co-worker, but Swithin who was chasing her. She vaulted over a bed, hoping to trip him up. But he hurdled over it too, gaining on her. Whoever knew that butlers were so athletic?

"Swithin, you idiot, grab her!" It was Max. By the nearness of his voice she could tell he'd followed them into the room. Had Hale? "And get that disk!"

Those last words spurred her feet to sail that last yard to the Eiffel Tower door, which she threw open and dashed through the same moment a wiry hand pinched down on her arm, yanking her backward. Swithin whirled her around, so that she was just in time to see Hale attempt to grab the gun away from Herbert—but the fat man was faster than he looked and whacked Hale across the face with the gun.

Cathy gasped. "No!"

With a loud smack on the back of the head, Hale was out cold. As he sank to the ground, any hope in her heart sank too. She made a move to run toward him, but Swithin twisted her arm painfully and bridling with indignation, she turned to face Max.

"You creep!" she spat.

Max laughed in her face for a moment before his jowls went slack and his beady eyes honed in on her ferociously. "Give me the disk."

Cathy swallowed. Hale had the disk the man was looking for, with the evidence that could convict him. All she had was…

Casting her eyes down, hoping not to give herself away, she reached into her handbag and pulled out another disk. It was a blank—she'd only had time to copy files onto the disk she'd given to Hale. Feeling a little sting of glee, she handed the blank disk over to Max Herbert. "You still won't get away with this," she said, hoping to God it was true.

He took her offering with a sneer. "My dear, you sound

achingly like something out of *Perils of Pauline*. Now let's move along.'' He clamped his hand down on the arm Swithin didn't have and the two began pulling her out the door.

Cathy dug her heels into the carpet. ''Where are we going?''

''For a ride,'' Herbert told her. ''A plane ride. Ever been to the Cayman Islands?''

''No.'' She could have wept. ''But it hasn't been for lack of trying.''

Their exit was stopped by Bernie. He was standing behind Bob, awkwardly holding a gun. ''What am I supposed to do?'' he asked, nodding toward Hale's inert form.

Cathy felt tears building in her eyes. Oh, Hale! She couldn't just leave him. But what choice did she have?

Max poked Cathy. ''We've got the girl and the disk. You stay here with the brothers Delaney. If either one tries anything funny, they'll have to drag the blue Caribbean for our young Miss Marple here.''

His words made Cathy's throat dry with fear, but she'd be damned if she'd let him see it. ''The name's Harriet,'' she snapped.

As Max shoved her down the hallway toward the elevator, she turned, struggling for a last glance at Hale. And Bob! She had nearly forgotten about him. He'd been innocent all along.

''Call the police!'' she yelled back at him. ''And help Hale!''

Bob's blue eyes blinking at her in surprise was the last thing she saw before she was dragged down the hall toward the emergency exit stairs.

''HALE?''

Hale's name felt like a hammer blow as it reached his

ears. He didn't have to be a rocket scientist to know some-one had slugged him, but he couldn't quite remember...

"Hale, can you hear me?"

He allowed one eye to squint open. The blinding light nearly convinced him to close it again, but then he focussed on the form hovering over him. Bob!

His brother poked his wire-rimmed spectacles up the bridge of his nose and blinked. "Are you all right?"

"Sure, aside from feeling as if I've just been slugged with a crowbar," he said. "What are you doing here?" Before Bob could answer, the scene from the hotel came back in a rush, and Hale shot up to a sitting position. "Where's Cathy?"

Bob wrung his hands. "I—I'm not quite sure..."

"Swithin," Hale said, remembering suddenly all that his brother had been through. "He kidnapped you?"

Bob nodded. "Bernie, Max, and Swithin had all planned to leave the country tonight, but when Swithin realized you had returned to Manhattan to help snoop around the bank, he panicked and took me with him, afraid I already might have figured out too much."

Hale rubbed his sore temple and frowned. "Who tossed Cathy's apartment?"

"Bernie did that. He wanted to know where Cathy and I had been headed for our honeymoon. When he found out we were going to the Cayman Islands, and might be onto him, he went a little nuts. I think he's been drinking—and unfortunately, he's all we're left with. After slugging you, Max Herbert and Swithin took Cathy and the computer disk that you two made."

Hale looked around, trying to sort things out. They were on the floor of a hotel bathroom, locked in, obviously. He reached into his pocket and felt the disk Cathy had handed to him mere moments before Max Herbert had made his appearance. His mind raced. He needed to get them out of there, quick, so he could go after Cathy. He had to get to her before Herbert discovered that she was lying about having the disk.

"You say Bernie's alone out there?"

Bob shook his head. "He's armed, Hale. I don't see what we can do..."

"You're his friend."

"*Was* his friend," Bob said, the sting of betrayal fresh in his voice.

"You still know how Bernie thinks. You say he's freaking out—but how would he hold up if he knew that he was facing jail?" He produced the computer disk and explained about the switch he and Cathy had pulled.

Within moments, Bob had coaxed Bernie away from Financial News Network on the television to the bathroom door. "You've got to let us out, Bernie," Bob explained through the door. "Hale says the disk that incriminates you all is already in the hands of the police."

"I don't believe it!"

"It's true. The disk Cathy had was blank, Bernie. If you help us, maybe the cops will be lenient."

There was a silence outside. Hale looked at Bob. If this didn't work, he fully intended to kick the door down and make a run for it.

Then, tentatively, Bernie asked, "How lenient?"

Hale smiled. "No jail time," he said. "Hell, if you help catch Max Herbert, who knows? You might not even lose your job at the FIB."

"They might even give you a promotion," Bob said when there was no answer. "If you're helpful."

From the silence from beyond the door, it didn't sound as if he was buying it. Hale smacked his fist against his palm in agitation. "I'm a cop, Bernie. I could convince the feds that this was all set up as a sting operation. They'd be happy to let you go if they could get a big fish like Herbert.''

"It's true," Bernie said nervously. "I'm just a little player. I didn't even steal that much money until Swithin came around and convinced me to take more…''

"Sure," Hale said, "no one wants to get you, Bernie. It's big-time operators like Max Herbert that they really want. Think how grateful the bank would be if you helped reel him in!''

Bob smiled. "I'm sure you'd make employee of the month," he told the man beyond the door.

Employee of the month decided it, apparently. Within moments, they heard a key inserted into the knob on the other side, and the door opened.

Hale immediately grabbed Bernie by the lapels and pushed his gangly frame against a wall. "Where is she!" he barked at the startled man. "Where the hell did Max Herbert take her?''

Bob, moving faster and with more assurance than Hale had ever witnessed in his brother, frisked his old friend and removed a small caliber handgun from his jacket. He held it stiffly. "You'd better tell us, Bernie."

Bernie nodded his head like mad and said, "Max has a plane at a private airport near here. Somerset Airport."

Bob looked at Hale. "The dummy accounts that they've set up from embezzled money are in the Cayman Islands.''

"I was supposed to go tomorrow, after everything here was taken care of," Bernie said. "I—I don't know why Swithin got to go and I didn't.''

"Maybe Herbert was setting you up as the fall guy," Hale told him. "Someone solid for the Treasury Department to pick on once your boss was safely out of the country. Did you ever think of that?''

Apparently he hadn't, because his face turned a sickly shade of green. "But I was the one in the bank risking his neck—or at least his job!"

Hale didn't have time to give Bernie a lecture about honor among thieves being a myth. Somewhere out there, a plane was about to take off with Cathy on it.

He shoved Bernie into the bathroom and was about to turn and lock him in when Bob pushed past him. To his surprise, his little brother landed a sharp blow to Bernie's temple, causing his traitorous friend to collapse to the floor in a heap.

"I hate to say it, but that felt good," Bob said, grinning.

While Bob locked Bernie in the bathroom, Hale ran to the phone and dialled 911. He wasn't taking any chances. He reported a kidnapping and sent the officers to the airport. Then he hung up the phone and sprinted for the door, dragging Bob behind him.

"Can the police arrest Herbert for embezzling?" Bob asked after Hale shoved him into a cab downstairs and barked out the airport name to the cabbie.

"Technically, no. But while he's being held on kidnapping it'll give me time to turn the disk over to the authorities. That way, the Treasury will have no trouble locating Mr. Herbert when they do want to press charges."

"Good thinking," Bob said.

It was, if the timing worked. Hale tapped his fingers nervously against the seat, cursing the speed limit. If they didn't get to the plane in time, the whole plan could fall apart. And Cathy could be lost to him forever.

10

"ARENT YOU GOING TO fasten your seat belt, Miss Marple?" Max asked as he stretched his own belt over his impressive bulk.

Cathy turned her head and pursed her lips at him across the aisle. "I don't see why that's necessary."

He grinned back, which made his double chin become a triple. "We're about to take off, my dear."

God, she hated him. Of course, she would have hated him even if he weren't so sneering and smug. Just this afternoon in Hale's arms she had been euphoric—if it weren't for this odious jerk and his slimy nephew, she might be still. Unfortunately, she seemed to have the bad luck always to be kidnapped when she was on the verge of happiness.

Nevertheless, she wasn't going to allow either Max or Swithin the satisfaction of seeing her discomfort. She lifted her chin proudly, single though it was. "This plane is not going to take off!"

At that moment, the engines revved and the twelve-seater airplane gave a lurch as it began to lumber toward the small airport's single runway, making her defiant announcement seem laughable. "I'm afraid you're wrong about that, my dear," Max said.

She glared at him, remembering the only bit of leverage that she had. The disk. She wasn't sure what he would do when he discovered that he'd actually left the evidence of his crimes behind. Would he stop long enough to go back and retrieve the real disk, or would he be even more eager to flee the country?

Apparently, she didn't have time to think it all out. As the plane continued its journey to the runway, she told him, "The only time I was mistaken tonight, Mr. Herbert, was when I told you about that disk."

His grin remained frozen in place. "What about the disk?"

"Check it," she said. "You might reconsider your plans."

Max turned to Swithin, who pulled a laptop out from under his seat and thrust the disk in question into it. After the computer whirred for a few moments, the man looked up at his uncle, mystified. "There's nothing on it!" he exclaimed. "It's blank!"

Max's face turned bullring red. He attempted to leap to his feet, but his girth was impeded by his seat belt. Cathy smirked, which only made him angrier. "Stop the plane!" he thundered as he fiddled with the belt's lock. "And get me that idiot Bernie Morton on the phone!"

"Goodness," Cathy taunted gleefully. "It wasn't Bernie's fault you foolishly took the disk without checking, was it?"

Max finally extricated himself from his seat and towered over her, fuming. "If anything goes wrong, your next career will be as shark bait!"

The anger on his face left no doubt that he meant his words. Swallowing hard, Cathy shut up.

"Bernie's not answering the phone, Max," Swithin said nervously from behind them. He'd been his usual cucumber calm self up till now, but Cathy could tell by the sweat beading on his brow that he was very nervous—especially at the prospect of their escape not going smoothly.

"Damnation!" Max cried. "I knew I shouldn't have left that little rotter in charge of things."

Cathy could only pray that Bernie's failure to answer his master's call meant that Bob and Hale had managed to pull something off. Please, God, let them be safe!

The pilot came forward. "Should we go back?"

"No!" Herbert screamed, causing the occupants of the small plane to wince. His eyes were bloodshot, and he tugged at the collar of his Savile Row shirt. "I mean, yes! Let Bernie take care of this ridiculous business."

"We can't leave evidence behind!" Swithin interjected with growing frustration. He tossed the infernal blank disk to the thin carpet covering the plane's floor. "I told you we should have left days ago, when we first had Bob locked away in Connecticut—but, no! *You* wanted to stick around for your *birthday party!*"

Max sent him a withering stare. "It had been planned for months. If *you* hadn't panicked and come to Atlantic City before I told you to, making the blunder of bringing Bob with you—"

Despite the threat of becoming a midnight snack for carnivorous marine life that lingered over her head, Cathy snickered at the two bickering Englishmen. "Sounds like Noel Coward meets Quentin Tarantino."

"Shut up, you!" Max bellowed.

Seeing the murderous fury in his face, Cathy quickly did as advised. The dramatic conclusions of *JAWS I, II* and *III* scrolled through her mind.

"We need to get Bernie to search the Delaney boys," Swithin said reasonably, with only a slight jeer as he mentioned his former employers. "It could be that they didn't have time to make a copy of the disk. Bernie said that Hale and the woman had only been in the hotel room a short time."

Max spun and fixed her with a glare. "*Is* there a copy?" he asked her.

Cathy gulped. If she said no, the plane would take off, but if she said yes, she might put Hale in danger. She didn't want anything to happen to him. Then again, she didn't want to spend the rest of her life tanning on Grand Cayman with these two mad dogs.

"She's not going to tell us the truth, you idiot!" Swithin howled disrespectfully to his uncle. "Why don't you use your noggin for once—we need to get out of here!"

Just when Cathy thought that punches might fly, she heard the squealing of tires careening across the wet asphalt of the runway. Through the window she saw the flashing blue-and-red lights of police cars encircling the plane. She leapt up. She was being saved!

"The police!" Swithin screeched. He ran up the aisle and, for some reason, grabbed Cathy. "What do we do?" he asked her, as if she and not his uncle were suddenly in charge. The panic in his eyes almost made her feel sorry for him. Almost.

Max took one look at the lights and bellowed at his pilot. "Get on the stick, Smith! Get us out of here."

"What should I do, run over the cops?" the pilot asked as he scrambled through the open passageway back to his seat.

Max grabbed Cathy's arm and yanked her away from Swithin. Cathy felt a flash of pain but suppressed a cry. "Tell whoever's at that tower that we have a hostage," he barked. "Tell them we take off or she dies."

Die? Cathy felt a wave of nausea.

Max dragged her up to the front of the plane, where the cops might see her through the windshield. The pilot, Smith, radioed the tower as requested. For at least five minutes, but what seemed like an eternity, nothing happened. Cathy's whole body seemed to tremble. And then, to her surprise, one of the police cars backed away, giving the plane enough room to pass.

They're letting us go? Cathy thought in horror. How could they do that? She craned her neck and saw a cab come speeding toward the plane. It screeched to a halt, and Hale and Bob jumped out of it as the plane lurched forward again. Hale was waving his arms and shouting at one of the officers.

Cathy wouldn't have thought her pulse could race any faster, but at the sight of Hale her heartbeat leapt like a team of huskies being mushed. No way was she letting Hale get out of her sight again! Herbert had her in his grasp, but she attempted to twist away, inadvertently brushing her rear against the control panel. The plane, like a giant steel balloon that suddenly deflated, flopped forward and sank to the ground with a metallic crash.

Chaos ensued. Herbert's considerable bulk went crashing into the copilot's seat, while Cathy fell back into the divider separating the pilot from the passengers. Landing in the aisle, Swithin let fly a string of colorful curses.

Knowing opportunity when she saw it, Cathy wasted no time sprinting for the emergency exit and pulling it open. While trying to get away from Max, she must have hit something on the panel that controlled the craft's landing gear, because the distance to the ground was significantly less than when she had boarded the plane. Swithin ran after her, and just as she was about to yell "Geronimo" and leap to the ground, he grabbed her arm.

"You've got to tell them," he babbled feverishly, "that I did nothing. I never saw any money! I was just the middleman, the go-between, the…"

The stoic had picked a fine time to have a nervous breakdown! She desperately needed to get off the plane, but the man wouldn't let go of her. He was so hysterical, he was like a drowning man who also drowns the person who could save him. Not that she had any intention of saving Swithin. In fact, as she looked behind him and saw Max staggering to his feet, she reeled in panic. She had to do something! Fast! Panicked herself, she yanked one of her arms free. Her left arm. It was then she remembered that Hale had called her Harriet Nelson.

She pulled back, said a quick prayer to the boxing gods, and let fly with a left hook. Miraculously, the punch landed squarely on blithering Swithin's bony jaw. The stunned man stumbled backward, leaving her free. Cathy turned, jumped to the asphalt and hit the tarmac running.

Hale was there in front of her, the wind riffling his black hair, and she ran to him as fast as her legs would carry her, her arms outstretched. When her head hit his chest, she knew what it was to feel safe; she never wanted to leave the shelter he offered her. Theirs was a regular Hallmark reunion, with the exception of the armed policemen surrounding them.

"Thank goodness you're all right!" Hale whispered in her ear.

Cathy looked into his blue eyes to answer, but at that moment an officer pulled them out of the way. An instant later, Cathy, still arm-in-arm with Hale, found herself face to face with Bob behind an EMS vehicle.

"Cathy!" Bob cried, oblivious to the fact that she had run into the arms of the wrong brother. "Thank heaven you're all right!"

The brothers seemed to be reading from the same script, but Cathy, feeling suddenly awkward, hadn't the slightest idea what to say next. She turned and saw Max Herbert coming off the plane, followed by Swithin on a stretcher, and the hapless pilot. The plane, which resembled a toppled steel bird, was surrounded by more cops than Fort Knox, all with their weapons drawn.

Hale gave Cathy another squeeze. "You did it, Cathy."

"I couldn't have done anything without you guys," she said, feeling almost detached, as if they'd just won a game of flag football instead of escaping with their lives from a dangerous situation. "If it weren't for you, I might be floating at the bottom of the ocean somewhere off the Cayman Islands."

As she spoke the name of her old honeymoon destination, she looked guiltily at Bob and shrank away from Hale's possessive embrace. She really needed to explain matters to her fiancé. After all, she and Bob should have been in the Cayman Islands *together* by now, had it not been for Hale and his father's intervention.

She and Bob looked back at Hale. He cleared his throat and was about to speak when a police detective named Saunders interrupted him. "Miss Seymour?"

Cathy stepped forward.

"We'll need you to come with us and make a statement," Saunders said. He looked over at Bob and Hale. "How do you two figure in?"

"I'm from the NYPD," Hale told him. "I called you guys."

"And I'm Miss Seymour's fiancé," Bob said for lack of anything more logical.

"*You* are?" the detective asked, looking from Bob to Hale to a blushing Cathy and then back again. Apparently, he'd witnessed Hale and Cathy's reunion on the tarmac. But when no one contradicted Bob's statement, he merely shrugged. "Okay, let's all go. One of you can ride with me and explain this whole mess."

Cathy glanced at Hale, hesitating. She needed to talk to

Bob, but she wanted to ride with Hale. She'd been through so much, she still craved the safety of his arms.

Hale watched her with interest. For the moment, she was still torn between two brothers. Apparently sensing her dilemma, he turned to Saunders. "I'll ride with you," he volunteered.

By his stiff carriage as he walked away with the detective, however, Cathy realized too late that Hale was hurt by her hesitation. But what did he expect her to do, she wondered with an irritability born of fatigue and frayed nerves, tell Bob right then and there that she wanted to call it quits?

"Shall we go?" Bob asked, taking her arm and escorting her toward another squad car.

Cathy nodded. Her body felt so numb. "I could use some coffee," she said.

"I'm sure we can get some at the station. I could use a cup, too," Bob said, looking at her closely.

Cathy shifted uncomfortably as she stared back at him, into eyes that were blue like Hale's, and yet without quirky humor or infuriating teasing that she had come to associate with the older Delaney brother…the brother she had, to her wonder, come to care for more than any other man in the world.

"Maybe we could find a place to talk, alone, at the station," Bob said. "I think we have some things to discuss."

Cathy nodded, praying silently that Bob wouldn't suggest getting married right away. Of course, that wasn't going to happen. It couldn't—not after what had happened between her and Hale in that hotel in Atlantic City.

Things to discuss? Did they ever!

"THE LONG AND SHORT of it is, I've discovered I need something more in my life. Something deep and meaningful.''

Cathy stared in bewilderment at Bob, whose pudgy hands were circled around a cup of stale, lukewarm police-station coffee. When they had found the break room of the station, she'd thought it would serve as a quiet, private place to tell Bob that they couldn't go on as before. She'd even been prepared to take off her engagement ring and give it back to him. But no sooner had Bob stirred the half-and-half into his coffee than he dropped this bomb on her.

''You mean *you* want to call off the wedding?'' she asked, unable to hide an indignant upward inflection. She hadn't expected this!

''I think it's best,'' Bob replied. ''You see, when I was sitting in that hotel room in Atlantic City with a gun pulled on me, I suddenly saw my life pass before my eyes—and I didn't like what I saw. Let's face it, Cathy, we've both gotten into a rut. Life should be more than routine, and trying to be just like everybody else, and dedicating your life to a bank.''

She nodded. ''Yes, but...''

He sighed. ''It's not that you're a dull person, Cathy. It's not your fault at all.'' He shrugged, and in that moment, Cathy wondered whether she *hadn't* been a dull person when she was with Bob. ''I just need a change.''

''What are you going to do?'' she asked him, but her subconscious was already racing with an equally compelling question: What was *she* going to do?

''I'm going back to Connecticut to work for my father.''

Her eyes widened in horror. ''Oh, no!'' She had accepted that a lot of what happened had been for the best—if Kevin Delaney had started a public investigation and implicated Bob to the authorities, it would have been very likely that Bernie Morton, Swithin, and Maxwell Herbert would have had time to clear their paper trail and head to Switzerland. She might never have met Hale. But she still resented the little dictator.

"I want to reconcile with him, Cathy," Bob told her. "I know he seems a little gruff…"

A little? "Yeah, and Stalin was a little mean!"

Bob smiled patiently. "Back at the house, he said if I wasn't involved in the theft that he would give me a job overseeing all his accounts, and I'm going to take it. He pays well, and maybe in ten years, I'll have the security of my inheritance and enough money amassed to retire and do what I really want."

"What's that?" She was appalled that she had absolutely no clue. How could she have been on the verge of marrying someone about whom she knew so little?

"Go to chef's school."

Cathy was stunned. Her first thought was how terrible it would be for Bob to spend so much time in a kitchen. His weight—his cholesterol! But then, she remembered. If Bob was calling their engagement quits, his cholesterol was none of her business. And what's more, it never had been. She had been trying to mold Bob into what she wanted, what she needed. She'd attempted to shape his life as rigidly as she had reshaped hers, and probably, it had felt to Bob as if she were about to drag him off to a prison in the suburbs. Maybe she had more in common with Kevin Delaney than she cared to admit.

"Do you have any plans?" Bob asked her as she twisted off her ring. "I mean, you must have gone through some change while you were being held hostage?"

She looked at him and felt her cheeks redden. Her biggest transformation hadn't taken place at gunpoint, but under a decorative mosquito net. She had fallen in love with her fiancé's brother. She had followed her own heart and let her dreaded free spirit loose…and just as she'd promised herself, she didn't regret a thing. She really didn't.

It was just… *Now* what was she supposed to do? She couldn't just saunter up to Hale and say, "Bob's history now, and, oh, by the way, are you free for dinner for the next fifty years?" She wasn't even certain that *she* was ready for fifty years with Hale, or even fifty days. After all, she'd been so careful with Bob, and look at how little she'd known him!

She slid her ring across the table. "I'm not sure…" Of anything. She had tried so hard to do things right, and what had her efforts amounted to? Maybe her dream life in the suburbs wasn't the be-all and end-all she had anticipated. It certainly hadn't worked out too well for Hale and Bob. Maybe normal wasn't all it was cracked up to be.

Bob opened his mouth to say something, but stopped when Hale stepped into the room. "Hey, you two," he said. "Been debriefed yet?"

Bob looked amazed. "Do you think they would want to hear my side of the story?"

"I don't see why not," Hale replied.

Bob, feeling newly important—and, Cathy feared, newly freed from her clutches—scooted out to find a policeman. Finding themselves alone at last, Hale grinned intimately at her and strolled over to pour himself a cup of coffee. Even when she looked away, she could feel those blue eyes pinned on her.

Cathy felt her cheeks redden. Why couldn't she be one of those women who never blushed?

"Soooooo…" Hale said.

She crossed her arms over her chest and slanted a stare at him. "Yes?"

He laughed. "Strange how awkward it feels, now that there's nothing to stop us."

She raised a brow. "Stop us from what?"

"You know…" He sent her one of those sexy grins that made her realize exactly what he meant. "Now that you and Bob are no longer an item, I just thought…"

At that startling and distressingly true statement of her engagement status, she hopped out of her chair. "What were you doing, listening at the door?"

He blinked. "No, of course not."

"Then how could you possibly know that Bob and I called off our engagement?"

"My brother told me."

But Bob had just left, and the two of them hadn't been alone together since she'd escaped from the airplane, so how… "Do you mean that Bob told you he was calling off our engagement before he told *me?*"

Hale, obviously sensing he'd blundered, shook his head. "He didn't actually say flat out that he was calling it off. I guess you might say that I inferred it from what he was saying that day at the house."

"At the *house?*" Cathy asked, her voice practically a squeak. "You mean you've known this for two whole days?" When all the events that had transpired in the past two days sprang to mind, she clapped her hands over her cheeks. "Why didn't you tell me?"

Seeing her reaction, he took a step closer. "I thought about it, but it wasn't my place."

"But even when we…made love…you knew? And you didn't tell me?" Why hadn't he?

"That was between you and Bob."

"But what was happening in that hotel room was between you and me," she argued. "Are you such a relationship-hater that you didn't want me to attach too much significance to our making love? Did you think if I didn't have Bob I would try to attach myself to you?"

Now it was Hale's turn to look red-faced and flustered. "You've got it all wrong, Cathy," he said, stepping forward again and taking her by the shoulders. "I *want* you to attach yourself to me."

"Ha!" This from the man who had sneeringly called her Harriet for two days!

"I know it sounds strange, coming from my lips, but I..." he took a deep, bracing breath "...I think we should..."

Cathy almost laughed. "Skippy Dewhurst had an easier time of it than you are."

"Listen to me, Cathy," he said, a bead of sweat beginning to form on his brow. "I'm not a Skippy Dewhurst. I didn't just want to have a one-afternoon fling with you. I think we should...should..."

Even as his grip on her shoulders tightened, words failed him. Cathy felt her hopes rise then fall in disappointment every time the words *we should* issued from his lips. The natural next words, such as, "get married," or, "have wild hotel sex more often," or even, "do lunch sometime," never followed.

"My goodness," she said in awe, as if she were a scientist observing a rare bug under a microscope, "you're so terrified of permanent relationships that you can't even come out with a good line when you need one."

He shook his head. "I *do* want a permanent relationship."

She studied him for a moment. He looked sincere, yet she felt so skittish inside, how could she trust that he meant what he said? After all, he'd only blurted it out when cornered. "So much has happened over the past two days, Hale. I need some time to think things through..."

He nodded. "Of course. If you want time, you've got

it.'' When she didn't respond, he tilted his head, a worried frown puckering his brow. "How much time, exactly?"

She moved away from him and gathered up her purse. If she stayed in the room much longer, she was likely to do something stupid, like jump into his arms, or agree to move to Brooklyn. "I'll call you," she promised, brushing past him on her way out the door, trying not to see the uncertainty in those deep blue eyes.

11

"YES, MY HAIR IS GREEN. Now what was it you wanted to talk about?"

Hale sank into the chair opposite Cathy's sister and fidgeted awkwardly. It wasn't just Joan's startling appearance that had him in knots, it was being in this position of needing advice. And sitting across a desk from someone whose nameplate read Joan Baez Seymour, Ph.D. failed to inspire confidence in her ability to fix his problem.

"It's not like I'm checking up on Cathy or anything like that…" he began.

Joan smiled knowingly and tapped her green lacquered fingertips against the black Formica of her kidney-shaped desk. "You just want to know how she is."

Hale frowned. He didn't want to be pushy. That night in the station, ten whole days ago now, Cathy had told him that she would call him once she had sorted things out a little better. She needed some time, she'd said. And he'd seen the logic in her words. But just how long did it take a woman to sort things out? Especially now that Bob was out of the picture. Hale had hoped she'd come to realize that she missed him. That, apparently, was not the case.

"I've been waiting for her to call me, but she hasn't." Hale sighed. Frankly, he didn't know what he was doing here. He stood. "But as long as I know that she's doing all right…" He turned and started walking toward the door.

"She's not," Joan said, stopping him halfway.

He spun on his heel.

"She's not fine, or okay, or anything approaching normal. In fact, my sister is a very sick woman."

Now he felt sick, too. "What's the matter with her?" he asked, already poised to dash to Cathy's side.

Joan steepled her fingers. "In my professional opinion, she's a nutcase—a quivering shell of her former self," she informed him. "Yesterday she was at my apartment and she did nothing but sigh and drink Red Zinger tea for three straight hours. I finally had to push her out the door before my nerves—and possibly her kidneys—gave out."

Hale rubbed his jaw. "That sounds worrisome."

"I've seen it before in patients. The listlessness, the misery, the lack of concentration. She's a zombie."

"What do you think is causing it?"

"Love." Joan pronounced her diagnosis as if it were a completely irrefutable scientific fact. "She's lovesick, in the most horrible kind of way. And it's all your fault."

Hale lowered himself back down into the chair, and slowly began to grin. Joan was smiling now, too.

"Should I go see her today?" he asked. "If I just talked to her…"

She shook her green head vehemently. "Whatever you do, don't talk. Cathy could talk herself out of anything. For years I tried to convince her that Bob wasn't the man for her, but did I get anywhere?" Joan shook her head. "Yet you succeeded in a matter of days where I failed. And you know how?"

"How?"

"Action. She needed to be jolted out of inertia—and right now she needs to be jolted again."

He took a deep breath. "I see…"

She frowned a big-sisterly warning. "But she doesn't

need to be led down the garden path. What Cathy wants is something permanent. It's what she's always wanted.''

Hale was shocked. ''But that's what *I* want,'' he protested. ''She thinks I'm some sort of bounder just because I live in a badly decorated apartment and don't live a suit-and-briefcase life like Bob and I've had a lot of girlfriends and…'' His voice trailed off. He didn't sound like a reliable prospect even to his own ears. ''But I've looked at things differently since I met Cathy.''

Was it so bad that he'd taken his time to realize he wanted something permanent in his life, like Cathy and a houseful of kids? After all, growing up in his father's house had left him domestically shell-shocked. But now he realized life with a family didn't have to be a rigid, smothering existence like the one he'd known as a child. He and Cathy would cobble together a future full of love and caring and compromise.

''I won't disappoint her,'' he promised her sister.

Joan stood. ''Good. Then I'll help you.''

He tilted his head and studied her. There was a devious glint in her eye. ''What did you have in mind?''

She grinned. ''Well, I've got a boyfriend named Duke— and I've heard that you've got a feisty dad who might come in handy…''

''You wanna go for Chinese?''

Cathy looked up at a group of co-workers poking their heads through the door of the office that had once belonged to Bernie Morton but now was all hers. She forced a smile, though she felt like weeping. As with everything else these days, Chinese food reminded her of Hale. ''Thanks, but I'm not hungry,'' she said.

''Suit yourself,'' they said, continuing their journey

down the hall. She heard their laughter as they waited for the elevator, and envied them their camaraderie.

Camaraderie reminded her of Hale.

After sighing over a cup of decaf for an hour, she decided a lunch break might be in order after all. She shut down her computer and went downstairs. In the lobby of the building her picture hanging on the wall by the entrance looked down at her. Her role in discovering Max Herbert's theft had earned her a promotion and the honor of being employee of the month.

But glancing even briefly at herself grinning crazily inside that frame, she saw that she looked as sickly and numb as she felt inside. Her life seemed to be on the brink of great change, yet she wasn't able to skip out of the groove she'd worn for herself over the course of a decade. Only now she didn't have Bob, and she hadn't as yet worked up the nerve to call Hale. To embark on a relationship with him seemed like plunging into the unknown. Yet not to embark on a relationship with him seemed like plunging into an abyss of bank loans, Lean Cuisines and lone movie matinees on weekends...

She exited through the bank's revolving door, rounded the corner by the deli, and nearly smacked into a man's broad chest.

"Okay, lady, come with me!"

Cathy sucked in her breath as his meaty hand clamped down on her arm. "Let me go! What are you doing?"

Tugging her toward a waiting cab, apparently. Cathy glanced at the yellow vehicle parked at the curb and dug in her heels. "Forget it, buster!" she shouted angrily. He gave her arm a wrench that was very effective. She stumbled alongside him a few steps. "I'm warning you—you won't get away with this! The last people who took me hostage are in jail now!"

Then it occurred to her—were these more of Max Herbert's men? Cold fear clawed at her heart. She'd assumed since Herbert was in jail awaiting trial that she was safe. But why shouldn't he and Swithin send someone out to get her?

She planted her foot against the car's open door, refusing to get in. "You tell your boss that I'm glad he's in the clink, and if he thinks he can just keep kidnapping people—"

"Tell him yourself," the man barked at her, giving her a shove that sent her reeling into the cab. She landed on the slippery vinyl seat with a thud and was followed in by the hulk himself, who shoved her onto the hump of the back seat.

There was another man in the back seat, too, wedged between her and the right back door. As the cab peeled into uptown traffic, Cathy looked at the small man and nearly let out a shriek of shock. Kevin Delaney! "I should have expected *you* would be at the bottom of this!" she said angrily. Maybe the goon who'd shoved her into the cab was his new butler.

His bearded face turned as red as hers, making him resemble Santa with a sunburn. "Don't give me any of your lip, lass!"

"Oh, why don't you leave me alone?" she huffed. "I was just minding my own business, going for a sandwich…"

"Oh, minding your own business, were you?" he taunted. "Were you minding your own business when you broke off your engagement?"

Her mouth dropped open in astonishment. "*I* broke off my engagement?" she repeated, stunned.

"That's what I said!"

"But I didn't," she clarified.

"All I know is, my son thought he was going to get married, and now he's *not* going to get married. And I'd like to know why the hell not."

He made it sound as if Bob had had nothing to do with the decision! "Why don't you ask him?"

"These youngsters never give straight answers!"

She rolled her eyes. Bob had probably told him what had happened twenty times already. The older man was incapable of hearing news that was inconvenient to him.

But maybe she could make him hear her. "Listen, you demonic little leprechaun," she said angrily. "Bob broke off our engagement over a week ago. *Bob* did it. But if he hadn't, I would have."

"Oh, you would have, would you?"

"Yes—and would you like to know why?"

He let out a dismissive grunt. "You couldn't say anything to interest me!"

Fine. She'd tell him anyway. "Because, you Gaelic grumpmeister, I'm in love with your other son—the one you disinherited for being a cop! The one who kidnapped me in the first place and helped find out who took all your damned money!"

They were whizzing down a highway somewhere in Queens, and it looked like they were headed for La Guardia. Fantastic. All she needed right now was an impromptu vacation!

Kevin glared at her. "Watch your mouth! You're talking to your future father-in-law."

Cathy thought she might tear her hair out. Or better yet, tear *his* hair out. The man refused to listen. "I am *not* getting married."

"Yes you are," he insisted.

"But I've told you and Bob has told you that it's all over. Accept it!"

He faced stubbornly forward, making her want to scream out her frustration. "Sure I don't know why anyone would *want* to marry you," he muttered.

She faced forward, too, deciding the best course of action was to remain silent and hope that she ran into a cop at the airport. Through the windshield she watched Queens pass by, then glanced briefly at the cab operator's name and photo I.D. Duke Rafferty. She wondered whether he would vouch for her when she told her story to the police. She memorized his number, then suddenly felt a pinprick of worry.

Duke Rafferty? Where had she heard of this guy before? Probably on one of those America's Most Wanted shows!

She looked up at his face in the rearview mirror, but his eyes were obscured by dark glasses, and a backward baseball cap covered his head. He wasn't familiar—but then, she'd met so many sterling characters lately, they were all beginning to blend together in her mind.

The driver pulled the cab up to the curb at the airport, and Cathy was escorted into the terminal. She, Duke, and the goon were preceded by Kevin Delaney, who strutted ahead of them, chest thrust forward as if he were leading a parade.

Cathy kept her gaze focussed on the metal detector ahead and the guards beside it, who gave her comfort. If she whispered a word about being a hostage and goons with guns, they would probably stop her.

"Hold it right there, Harriet," a familiar deep voice said.

From out of a gift shop strolled Hale, followed by Joan, and Bob. Cathy nearly collapsed with relief when she saw them. Semisane people! But most of all, she felt her legs wobble beneath her when her gaze met Hale's. He was dressed in a tux, and even though it wasn't exactly appropriate attire for La Guardia during noon rush, he looked terrific. His blue eyes glinted with warmth and humor and a passionate intensity that made her fear she would melt into a puddle right then and there. She shook off the goon's embrace and ran forward to greet him, feeling as she ran that she had just skipped out of that groove she was in.

"Hale!" she cried, launching herself against his chest. She didn't care who was watching. She'd missed him so much she'd ached with loneliness for over a week. She wasn't going to let another second go by without letting him know how she felt.

She was immediately gathered up in the tightest hug and sweetest kiss she'd ever experienced. His lips were warm and giving and reassuring, telling her all she needed to know about how much he'd missed her. When they finally came up for air, Hale clasped both her hands. "Cathy, I'm so sorry—that night at the police station there was so much I wanted to say, but I couldn't find the right words. And now…"

Her eyes glistened as she looked up at him, and her heart beat a quick tattoo of anticipation. But apparently, words weren't coming to him easily now, either. "It doesn't matter," she said. "You don't have to say anything, Hale."

"But I do," he said, dropping to one knee. "Otherwise, how will you ever know that I want to be Ozzie to your Harriet?"

She gasped. What was he saying? Did he mean…

His hands clasped hers more tightly. "Will you marry me, Cathy?"

Cathy felt tears well in her eyes. She'd been so caught up in the wonder of seeing him again that she'd completely forgotten about Kevin Delaney's insistence that she was soon to be his daughter-in-law. She'd thought he was going to try to force her to marry Bob! "You want me to marry *you?*" she asked, surprised.

His expectant smile faded, and for the first time, doubt clouded his expression. And no wonder. He was on his knees in a tux in front of a bunch of strangers headed for Disneyland and Topeka and Phoenix!

She laughed, and quickly moved to reassure him. "Of course I'll marry you!" she said, pulling him to his feet. "When? How soon?"

In answer to her questions, Joan bustled forward, holding a suitcase and two tickets. "That's all figured out," she interjected. "You're going to Vegas, and you'll have to hurry if you're going to make your five o'clock appointment at the True Love Chapel. Elvis will be your minister."

Cathy took the bag and her ticket and blinked back the moisture from her eyes. She hugged Joan, and Bob, and Duke, and accepted their best wishes with unending gratitude. She didn't know how many people were in cahoots in all this, but she loved them all. Except maybe...

She turned to Kevin Delaney. "For your information, I've reconciled with *both* my sons," he told her. "Though I don't know why in the world a nice boy like Hale would have to cast his lot with a mean-tempered banshee like yourself."

Cathy couldn't help it. At this moment, she even loved *him.* She laughed, and placed a kiss on his bearded cheek. Kevin Delaney turned a bright pink, and looked for a brief moment as if he might be a wee bit pleased with the way things had turned out with his sons.

All her life, Cathy had been running from her flaky family. But standing in that airport, flanked by some of the craziest relatives the world could know, she began to have an inkling of the upside of being permanently attached to a select group of oddballs. Yes, they could make you the laughingstock of your elementary school, and a nervous wreck as an adolescent, and could even run off to Guatemala, leaving you orphaned. But as Cathy gave her green-haired sister a last hug, she knew she would be eternally thankful for one relative who had always stood by her when she was at her absolute stubborn worst, and stepped in when she needed her most.

In fact, she'd always thought her parents had done everything wrong, but now she finally appreciated one thing they had done very right. "If I ever have a daughter," she told Joan, "I'd want her to be just like you."

Joan gaped at her skeptically through moist eyes. "Hair color and animal prints notwithstanding?"

"Of course!"

"Your husband might have something to say about that," Joan joked.

Dashing away a tear, Cathy turned to Hale, looked into those blue, blue eyes that had first snagged her attention, and felt her heart swell almost to the bursting point. Husband? It seemed too good to be true.

He took her hands in his, smiling, but looking a little worried at the same time. "We can move anywhere you want, Cathy. I'll shower you in white picket fences."

His words almost made her weep again. "Will you man the barbecue grill for the July Fourth picnics?"

He sent her a devastatingly sexy grin. "You bet. I'll even wear an apron that says Kiss the Chef on it."

She laughed. "I'm sure you'll have plenty of takers."

As he gazed at her lovingly, the look in his eyes turned almost shy. "I'm serious, Cathy. We can go house hunting as soon as we get back."

She hugged him tight, loving him for wanting to compromise with her, for wanting to give her one part of her dream. But all her old desires didn't seem so important now that she had Hale—he was what she'd never expected—a genuine dream come true. "Why don't we just hang out in Manhattan for now, and have fun, and see how it goes."

He lips turned up in a grin, but his eyes registered worry. "Are you feeling all right, Cathy?"

She laughed. "Never better! Now let's go get married!"

They waved goodbye to their entourage one last time and made their way to the line to pass through the metal detectors.

"I've been going crazy without you," Hale confessed, once they were alone.

Cathy felt a shiver as he whispered in her ear. "I'm so glad," she replied. "I'd hate to think that I was the only one who was miserable."

He laughed. "You had company, you just didn't know it."

Seeing that grin of his again, which had haunted her dreams for ten whole days, she decided she couldn't keep her hands off him for another minute. She threw her arms around him and gave him a hug before walking through the metal detector. She couldn't wait for them to be husband and wife—all they had to endure was a flight across the country and a wedding ceremony before they could be together, forever. Life was perfect. Nothing could stop them now.

Hale stepped through the metal detector and set off the alarm, which beeped insistently even after he'd thrown his keys in a plastic bowl and walked through again. So much for nothing stopping them! Cathy felt a moment of panic as he stood looking sheepishly at her, until he suddenly remembered something and pulled a small square box out of his jacket's breast pocket. He flashed the ring at the guard as explanation, then stepped forward to Cathy.

"I forgot—this is for you," he said, showing her the diamond solitaire set exquisitely on a braided gold band.

He raised his brows comically. "I thought maybe if the ambush and the tux didn't do the trick..."

"That I could be swayed by jewelry?" She smiled, plucked the ring off its satin pillow and slipped it on her finger, where it fit perfectly, as if meant to live there.

He shrugged impishly. "Well...I thought one traditional gesture was in order. I know you like to do things by the book."

"That was before I was kidnapped three times, and discovered the joy of wigs, green wrap dresses, and jumping out of airplanes." Cathy reached up and planted a very sensual, very public kiss on his lips that didn't end until several antsy travellers in the backed-up line behind them made the guards move the soon-to-be-newlyweds along.

"We'd better hurry," she said with a wink for her brand-new fiancé. "Elvis awaits."

Take 2 bestselling love stories FREE

Plus get a FREE surprise gift!

Special Limited-Time Offer

Mail to Harlequin Reader Service®

3010 Walden Avenue
P.O. Box 1867
Buffalo, N.Y. 14240-1867

YES! Please send me 2 free Harlequin Love & Laughter™ novels and my free surprise gift. Then send me 4 brand-new novels every other month, which I will receive months before they appear in bookstores. Bill me at the low price of $2.90 each plus 25¢ delivery per book and applicable sales tax if any*. That's the complete price, and a saving of over 10% off the cover prices—quite a bargain! I understand that accepting the books and gift places me under no obligation ever to buy any books. I can always return a shipment and cancel at any time. Even if I never buy another book from Harlequin, the 2 free books and the surprise gift are mine to keep forever.

102 HEN CH7N

Name	(PLEASE PRINT)	
Address	Apt. No.	
City	State	Zip

This offer is limited to one order per household and not valid to present Love & Laughter™ subscribers. *Terms and prices are subject to change without notice. Sales tax applicable in N.Y.

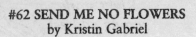